AF539034

The burden of FOREKNOWLEDGE

Born and brought up in the hot, dusty plains of Uttar Pradesh, Jawahara Saidullah credits her love of writing to too-frequent power cuts and no television. With a Master's degree in Communications, Jawahara currently works as a computer book editor though she has been a college instructor and a technical writer in other incarnations. Her work has appeared in several publications, including the recent Seal Press anthology *Voices of Resistance.* She was a weekly columnist for *Mid-Day* in Mumbai and is a regular columnist for www.chowk.com. Jawahara divides her time between Boston and Geneva with her husband and a very spoilt dog named Naina.

OTHER INDIAINK TITLES :

A.N.D. Haksar	*Madhav & Kama: A Love Story from Ancient India*
Boman Desai	*Servant, Master, Mistress*
C.P. Surendran	*An Iron Harvest*
I. Allan Sealy	*The Everest Hotel*
I. Allan Sealy	*Trotternama*
Indrajit Hazra	*The Garden of Earthly Delights*
Jaspreet Singh	*17 Tomatoes: Tales from Kashmir*
Kalpana Swaminathan	*The Page 3 Murders*
Kamlini Sengupta	*The Top of the Raintree*
Madhavan Kutty	*The Village Before Time*
Pankaj Mishra	*The Romantics*
Paro Anand	*I'm Not Butter Chicken*
Paro Anand	*Wingless*
Paro Anand	*No Guns at My Son's Funeral*
Ramchandra Gandhi	*Muniya's Light: A Narrative of Truth and Myth*
Ranjit Lal	*The Life &Times of Altu-Faltu*
Rashme Sehgal	*Hacks and Headlines*
Raza Mir & Ali Husain Mir	*Anthems of Resistance: A Celebration of Progressive Urdu Poetry*
Sharmistha Mohanty	*New Life*
Shree Ghatage	*Brahma's Dream*
Susan Visvanathan	*Something Barely Remembered*
Susan Visvanathan	*The Visiting Moon*
Tom Alter	*The Longest Race*

FORTHCOMING TITLES :

Anjana Basu	*Black Tongue*
Kalpana Swaminathan	*The Gardener's Song*
Prafulla Roy trans. John W. Hood	*Freedom's Ransom*
Selina Sen	*A Mirror Greens in Spring*
Shandana Minhas	*Tunnel Vision*
Susan Visvanathan	*Seine At Noon*

The burden of FOREKNOWLEDGE

JAWAHARA SAIDULLAH

IndiaInk
ROLI BOOKS

I*ndia*I*nk*

© Jawahara Saidullah, 2006

All rights reserved. No part of this publication may be reproduced or transmitted, in any form or by any means, without the prior permission of the publisher.

First published in 2006
I*ndia*I*nk*
An imprint of
Roli Books Pvt. Ltd.
M-75, G.K. II Market
New Delhi 110 048
Phones: ++91 (011) 2921 2271, 2921 2782
2921 0886, Fax: ++91 (011) 2921 7185
E-mail: roli@vsnl.com; Website: www.rolibooks.com
Also at
Bangalore, Mumbai, Kolkata, Varanasi, Agra, Jaipur

Cover Design: Nitisha Mehta
Page Layout: Kulvinder Singh

ISBN: 81-86939-31-8

Typeset in Garamond by Roli Books Pvt. Ltd. and printed at Anubha Printers, Noida (U.P.).

For Bijoy who makes me
believe…every day

CONTENTS

Acknowledgments

Writing is often talked about as a lonely process. But I had the support of too many people to believe that premise. The first person on my list is my husband, Bijoy, who never let me quit and gave me frank, sometimes even unflattering criticism to help me become the writer he believed I could be. I love him for that and everything else. I want to thank my parents and siblings for bearing with me through the years and for understanding how important being lost in strange characters and imaginary places were for me. Thanks to my mother-in-law Jamuna Varma and my sister-in-law Sajana, for being supportive and loving throughout this process. Behind my love of writing is also a fierce teacher, Mrs Roga, who taught me to trust in my voice and believe in my writing when I stepped into her classroom, a quivering bundle of nerves. I would like to thank Renuka Chatterjee, my very patient and very thorough editor. Thanks to the whole Roli team without whose tireless efforts we would not be holding *Burden* in our hands. I could not have made my final edits without endless cups of tea supplied by my niece, Laila. And, of course, thanks to Naina, who kept my toes warm and barked unrelentingly when she decided I had spent too much time hunched over the computer.

1

Changing Course

Zameerpur, Monsoon, 1567

My life lurks in the shadows. I see it in the erratic flickers of an oil lamp whose dancing flame plays changing, silhouetted tableaux on a rough earthen wall. It is a wall I have not seen or touched since I was snatched up, struggling and crying, and thrust midstream into a life that was not mine. I have searched for my life in many ways, sifting through possibilities, hopes and unspoken desires, like grains of sand on a river bank.

The Ganga changed its course and drowned my world, capturing me within its whirling eddies, even as I thrashed and tried to escape. The floodwaters swelled, feeding the river's fury until it crashed through the old earthen dam that had restrained it for over a century. I heard the crack, a million whips whistling, cutting through the angry flashes of lightning and the passionate rage of the thunder, and knew that all was lost.

The others in my village did not know anything until it was too late for escape. By then the village and all who lived in it had become a part of the river forever, trapped within its treacherous whirlpools. The river rampaged through our homes and fields and claimed them as her spoils. She was a ferocious, churning, muddy, marauding army that looted everything away from me, in an instant. My home, my parents, my friends… my life.

My village, Zameerpur, lush with rich dark soil, was the fertile gift of the Ganga. Its fields of bountiful, rippling gold, my home, the cradle of my childhood and early womanhood – I remember it in flashes. Each flash bursts within me, an image that has been burned into a corner of my mind, indelible yet incomplete, tantalizingly reachable yet just out of my grasp.

Zameerpur was as flat as the palm of my hand and just as brown and golden with the Ganga running alongside it like a lifeline. Ganga, the source of our abundance, our inspiration, our mother; patient, loving and permanent until one day when pent-up rage spilled over and she showed us who she really was, shattering our naïve assumptions.

~

I sit by the river on the horizontal branch of the old neem tree that grazes the water. I swing my legs down, dipping them into her coolness as I do every day through the hot summer months. This is my own place where I can escape my chores, my mother, my friends, and think about my life. This is where I talk to Ganga as if I know her, as if she can understand me. Already I know my destiny is commingled with hers.

I live every day with the burden of foreknowledge. Of knowing things before they happen, of being unsurprised by most events and people. It presses down upon my chest and heart until I feel I cannot take another breath. I know how all this will end and the certainty fills me with dread and foreboding.

But it was not always like this. For while I bore the mark of one who senses the future, I still had no idea of the heaviness of its burden. It was just a useful trick, to help my father and impress my friends.

I could tell my father whether the rains would be plentiful that year or if we were due for a drought. I knew if the banks of the river would overflow and if the fields would be full and bountiful. I was the daughter of farmers.

Farmers were forever dependent on the weather, for the food we ate and the conversation that sustained us. Depending on the weather we rejoiced or mourned.

I had another gift, although my parents considered it a burden in a girl poised at the cusp of puberty, not yet dispatched to her husband's home. It was a gift better suited to old, wrinkled grandmothers and village eccentrics. I always spoke my mind. My parents loved me and tried to beat it out of me. Somehow this task always fell to my mother. Stories of my troublesome tongue gave everyone something to talk about.

'Hey, your new husband looks like a monkey,' I had told one bewildered bride, making her burst into tears.

'The cows that ate your crop, last week? They're your neighbour Raghu's,' I informed an irate farmer. Incidents such as these could spark family feuds that lasted several generations. The reason might be lost to time, but the hatred between families would continue. This feud, however, lasted only a few months; it too was swept away along with everything else.

'Why did you say that? Why?' my mother asked as she hit my cheek with an open hand.

'Because it was the truth,' I wailed, inviting the whole village to witness my chastisement.

One old woman tried to intervene. 'What are you doing? Are you going to kill the child? Let her go.' She tried ineffectually to stall my mother's hand, deflecting the next blow.

The slap landed on my head, instead of my cheek, and I wailed even louder.

'Who do you think you are? Always telling people the truth. What business is it of yours?' A few more well-aimed slaps found their mark, making my face throb with pain.

'You told me to always tell the truth,' I shouted back between sobs. A few in the crowd chuckled and the beating stopped.

I had won.

~

The loo is a wind that fells grown men, killing the unwary and unprepared in an instant. Remaining outside for long periods, unprotected against its assault, causes burning fevers and nausea that lead to death. Those who survive, and there are a few, can only babble about the searing heat that burrows inside them until they feel it blossom into a tight, painful flower of fire and they know they will surely die.

When the loo blows, it brings with it the heat of the desert and its gritty sand, driving people indoors for refuge. I go out to feed our cows and it slithers up my nostrils until I choke. I gasp for breath trying to suck in the thin, super-heated air. It is as if a fiery serpent is trying to make its home inside me.

Just as I think I cannot bear it any more, I stumble back inside. The wind haunts us for days, whistling and whining like an angry, vengeful ghost. If I venture outside I wind a wet cloth around my head as I feed the cattle or help my mother draw water from the well in the courtyard.

The nights bloom clear and black and I can see each star etched into the sky, precise and silver. We sleep outside, my parents and I. I wait for that one isolated moment when a sudden cool breeze sweeps over my skin, leaving me yearning for another gust. I inhale the scents of the small, white flowers of the Queen-of-the-Night that the end of day forces into bloom. They will be dead by sunrise, their perfume spent, their petals bruised and rusted.

There are nights when my mother sits on my bed and lays my head on her lap. Sometimes she strings white flowers into strands and winds them into my hair and around my neck. I feel her rough hands on me, scented with the faint fragrance of the flowers, and drift slowly into sleep. She never talks, just lets her love envelop me and lull me towards drowsiness. Sometimes I grasp hold of her hand and refuse to let her leave. In the morning I find her sleeping in an uncomfortably twisted position, half on and half off the bed, her hand still clasped in mine.

The fields are ploughed, the seeds sown and now they await the rains. The wells have dried up and the river is a muddy trickle. By this time the rains should have irrigated the fields, washing away the layer of dry topsoil and feeding the thirsty roots. But there is nothing except the harsh whistle of the wind, taunting the sky-cast eyes of the farmers. They still set out, wet cloths wound around their heads, carrying precious water to drink from their wells. There is little to do except scare off a few emaciated, half-dead birds and the vultures that circle them. The earth cracks like a dry, leprous hide as the sun blazes fire and turns everything to a powdery dust. Eventually, the farmers decide to stay home until the rains arrive. We pray and wait. Nothing more can be done.

My father stands at the edge of the courtyard, eyes shaded by one hand as he gazes upwards.

'If it does not rain, there will be no harvest this year,' he mutters as he squints against the strength of the unshaded sun. The sky is a blinding blue, bright and cruel.

'It will rain Baba,' I tell him confidently. He smiles at me as always, the darkness fading a little from his eyes.

'Are you a girl or a weather vane?' my mother asks impatiently. I did not hear her come up behind me and I sidle away in case she decides to follow her question with a slap.

'Her husband is coming to get her in two weeks. And she is telling her father about the weather,' she mumbles, barely under her breath.

My father smiles again and we exchange a knowing glance. My mother continues her grumbling. She is nervous. Sending a daughter to her husband's house for the first time is serious business. I know this. I have known little else. She has been preparing for this day since I can remember. I do not even recall a time when I was not married.

I have forgotten my wedding. I was a child, of perhaps four, when my husband and his family arrived in their wedding procession to our house. My father tells me I fell asleep during the long ceremonies. Later, I stole my new husband's fancy turban and would not give it back to him. He cried loudly, rubbing his fists into his eyes with anger, as I ran around the house, unravelling his pretty headgear.

Now as I step over into womanhood through the door of puberty it is time to take the place that is mine and depart for my new home. My mother has been teaching me to cook, to sew, to be a farmer's wife. There is only one thing she has not succeeded in teaching me, to hold my tongue.

I am fourteen, soon to be fifteen, old enough to be a wife and a mother. I test out the words on my tongue, feeling their unfamiliar weight, their unreal taste in my mouth.

~

The wind has changed direction. It whispers now of the sweetness of the snow from the northern mountains. It tastes pure and cool as I inhale it and try to forget what I know is going to happen.

The clouds that roll in from the north are dark, hugely swollen with rain, crowding out the sun and dampening the blue of the sky. They hover for days, teasing us with the promise of rain, until they are vanquished by the sun's fire and are burned away into insubstantial wisps. But new ones arrive soon, densely black, pregnant with moisture and I know this time they will fulfil their promise. My friends and I prepare for the rain with excitement. We gather rope and wooden planks and make swings on the branches of the mango trees and sing timeless songs of the season of love.

O black cloud of saawan
And winds that blow this way
Lift my hair, flirt with me
But never can you stay.
For once my lover arrives
There is no you and me
Just him... Just him
For me.

I hum the tune for days, dreaming of my faceless husband who will soon be more than a face, more than a name, more than a body. As I sweep the yard, I feel wetness on the back of my hand. Another spot joins the first and my hand is drenched as is the rest of me. Drop follows heavier drop until the individual beads of water are indistinguishable in the downpour. The dry soil baked hard and arid by the sun drinks thirstily like a greedy child, too quickly, too soon. I complete the rest of my chores with greater speed than my mother would like and make my way to the swing.

Through the fluid curtain of the rain I see the flock of peacocks that live by the river spread their wings. With a flourish the largest male fans out his plumage, stretches his neck to the sky and dances with joy, the brilliant blue of his breast shot through with skeins of gold and purple glinting at me through the rain. The peacocks dance madly, as if the rain intoxicates them, fills them with joyous ecstasy, as if they cannot stop their feet from dancing, or their feathers from swaying and dipping. I laugh as I incline my face to the skies and let the rain wash over and into me, saturating every pore, invading every sense. I store away the memories of that instant as I prepare for everything to be snatched away. The large peacock sounds his harsh cry as if responding to my laughter and sashays away majestically into the grey mist rising from the river.

Saawan is here, the monsoon, the season of love and romance, and lust. I feel sensations explode in the tightening of my body. With each glide of the swing I soar upwards and touch the sky. Then I slow myself down, rocking gently, suspended in a lazy rhythm. My hands explore new curves as my clothes are plastered to my skin and I feel the sensuousness of the rains wash away my childhood.

~

It rains for two weeks without stopping. The crops, once in danger of a dry death, now lie rotting in the earth. The roof of our hut leaks and the mud walls see min danger of collapsing as the water soaks into them, trying to reclaim them for the earth. The sound of the rain becomes a dull backdrop to our lives until we can hear it no longer. The rain, the intermittent flashes of lightning and the prolonged angry bass of the thunder become the background against which we try to live. New clouds keep marching in, reinforcements to the spent and depleted ranks, and my sense of foreboding grows steadily, until I can think and feel little else.

'Baba, we must leave,' I say to my father as I hand him his tobacco pipe.

'This is our home.' He runs his fingers through my hair.

'We must. All this will go away. I feel it.' I persist, my voice shaking with fear.

'No, child. We have drought and we have flood. We have had rains… floods like this before. That is the life of farmers. You know that. You told me it would rain and it did. You just did not tell me how much it would rain.' He tries to make me laugh.

'This is different,' I say.

'Where would we go?' he asks, his tone letting me know that our conversation was over.

I tried. I really did. I argued and cajoled and cried. But we had no place to go. Besides, destiny is predetermined and I could not change it. My foreknowledge lay within me like a heavy stone dragging me down into the murky depths of a dark fear.

~

Today was to be my gauna, the day I would have entered my husband's home. Both his village and mine are marooned islands, isolated and alone, waiting for the final push when the Ganga will devour them and others around them. My parents talk of sending a messenger to discuss a new date once the waters have receded. I know this will never happen.

I wear the pink wedding sari my mother had bought years ago. It had been kept away for me, waiting for this occasion, in a chest protected and perfumed by the dried leaves from the large neem tree that grows in our yard.

I touch the embroidered golden flowers, tracing their raised ridges with one finger, and look at myself in the faded mirror. The darkness of the day outside casts strange shadows upon its dulled surface. The shadows play on my face and I look as if I belong in another time, another place. The kajol outlining my eyes makes them glow like twin lamps. The gold nose ring melts into the colour of my skin. Using my mother's ivory comb I untangle my hair, making it fall in black waves around me. Outside, in the small covered courtyard, I can hear my parents complain about the floods and the wind and the crops. I glance at myself again as I cover my hair with the sari and lower my eyes. I look like a bride.

The cold fear in my heart makes me sweat and I wipe away the beads from my forehead with the pallu of my wedding sari. And I wait for what I know must happen.

A gust of wind whips the sari off my head and blows my unbound hair across my face. The nearby dam that has tried its best to tame the river for years has been shattered. The sound echoes in my ears, reverberating, filling all the chambers in my head, until I feel as if I am fragmenting into nothingness. It makes the roar of the maddened water as it triumphs over the world sound dull in comparison.

The dingy white, almost grey curtains at the window behind me billow wildly before being torn off and flying away like a giant bird. Screams and cries echo all around me and are drowned almost instantly. I open my mouth to shout for help, instinct overcoming knowledge, and swallow a huge gulp of muddy water. I splutter and cough as the Ganga enters my room, engulfing it and carrying away everything that is mine.

There is no ground beneath my feet. I try to stay afloat as the river whips me around. Frantically I look for my parents who had been sitting in the courtyard just a moment ago. The courtyard is gone, taking them with it. I see the hut being dashed into tiny pieces by the liquid fury in which I am trapped. Flying debris hits my forehead and opens a gash. The blood is washed away almost instantly but the pain burns a hole through me. Thunder roars like a maddened beast and lightning splinters the sky.

Terror claws my insides like a sharp-taloned bird as I am cast adrift in a world of nightmares. Ganga, to whom I had whispered my hopes and dreams and desires, Ganga my secret confidante, has become an insane, violent torrent, intent on claiming me and everything around me. As the flood gathers fury and the rain batters me mercilessly, I see the low-flying flock of peacocks making their escape.

They are not graceful in flight, their crowns flattened and the colourful feathers tucked away, flying low over the water, almost skimming the churning surface. I reach out my hand mutely, asking for help, and brush against the large male. He flutters and flies upward in panic, leaving one of his feathers in my hand. A round golden eye surrounded by green and blue stares back at me. My hands seize with cold as I clutch the feather and I feel a wet chill seep into my bones, into every recess of my body.

I see a flailing goat, eyes wide with fear, float by. Its legs churn the water uselessly and its bleating echoes eerily. Then I see it go under and all is silent except for the storm. I tread water, exhausted yet hanging on to consciousness with all the strength I possess. 'Amma, Baba,' I cry over and over again, knowing it is useless and that they are gone. My voice grows hoarse and dies away. Some hard object strikes my head again and consciousness slips away from me in a thin trickle.

2

Kashi: City of the Dead

Kashi, Summer, 1568

The city of the dead comes alive at night. As the light of day dims and stars flower in the purple-black sky, the leaping flames of the funeral pyres respond by turning night into a perpetual twilit haze. Together the stars and the fires blaze in the not-quite-dark night. The smoke from the pyres creates gossamer realities that lie suspended between this life and the next.

I have lived here, in this ancient city, for months now, time passing by in a haze. Sometimes I can remember each minute detail of my life in Zameerpur as if it were yesterday. I can feel the teeth of the comb as my mother untangled my hair. I can feel the damp breeze that rose from the river at night and played upon my skin. I can see the fields rippling like rivers of gold. I can smell the fetidly sweet smell of the sugarcane juice being boiled for jaggery. I can feel the sensation of each raindrop touching my skin and sliding down my body. Then it all slips away.

These moments of remembrance are intercepted by periods in which I see Zameerpur as if through a murky fog, through which the passage of time is distorted and stretched out and the city of the dead becomes the only concrete reality of my life. Kashi is a maze of tangled streets and narrow by-lanes, secretive alleys and large temples. Every path, wherever it originates, leads to the river, which bounds the city from one side. The shore, where Ganga meets Kashi, is its throbbing, beating heart, which pulsates in a strange rhythm day and night. Life and death are gripped in a macabre dance by the river, each holding the other in check, balancing out existence.

As far as I know I am the sole survivor of the five drowned villages. The scar on my forehead, etched into my hairline, reminds me of home. That, the gold wedding nose stud I wear, a peacock feather and the tattered square of pink, wedding silk I carry close to my body. I warm the metal of the stud with my touch, caress its smooth surface and dream of my life as it had been, as it could have been. Carefully I open the folded square of pink and gold cloth. I touch the peacock feather that had remained clutched in my hand during my journey in the river. The feather is bedraggled, its shape flattened and mangled, its colours dulled and washed out. Still it is a touch of home, of my past, of my life. I drag it across my skin and relive the day when the peacocks flew low overhead, above the raging Ganga.

The Ganga had changed course that terrible day. It consumed my village and four others, swallowing them in one gulp. Sometimes I still dream that I swim down to murky depths and find my village, my parents and my childhood, perfectly preserved, trapped within the silky tendrils of a giant water hyacinth. I try to free them from its web and hear shouted words of encouragement, urging me to hurry.

Then I am caught, getting more and more entangled in the silken tendrils as I thrash and struggle to escape. I try to scream as I am dragged down. Down into the depths of darkness. I struggle to breathe and water floods my nose and mouth, burning through me like fire.

The people I meet in Kashi marvel that I survived when all others have perished. They wonder how I remained protected from the strong undertow and from the mounds of rocks and trees that could tear a body into shreds. I can give them no answers. Somehow I slipped unharmed through the debris, floated past the wreckage of many lives and was transported for miles, battered and barely conscious, flowing with the river, downstream toward Kashi. I was rescued by a fisherman on his way back home to the city. The people here tell me that I was clinging to a floating corpse when I was found. A poor anonymous woman whose life had been taken by the river had become my raft to safety. I remember nothing of this. I only know what I am told.

Kashi is the refuge of souls, the place where people come to die, for from here they are assured a safe, unobstructed passage to heaven. I wonder sometimes if I am already dead. I know for sure that at least a part of me has died.

~

I wander through the passageways of this house I live in. It is owned by the Dom Raja of Kashi and I am now part of his compound full of misfits and outcastes. I have never seen him but already I know who he is. As the most powerful man in the city, I, the River Girl, had been brought to him. Everyone calls me that, River Girl, because I have not told them my name. I cannot bear to say it out aloud.

I was unconscious when they brought me to him. He took me in, gave me a roof over my head and food to eat. His presence lives in every pore of the city. His name is spoken in whispers of awe and disgust and reverence and fear. Though he wears no crown and cannot even dream to be in the company of royalty, his will rules over the city. He is an untouchable, though so powerful that the city would flounder and be lost without his presence. He is its financial centre and he is the reason that people come to die in Kashi, the reason the living bring their dead to the city, the reason the economy of the city thrives. The Dom Raja is the scion of an unbroken line, whose untouchable yet strangely divine hands have helped many souls on their way to heaven. He takes his responsibilities seriously. Anyone who is desperate enough to seek his help is not turned away. The refuse of Kashi, its disenfranchised, lost souls find a place to rest in his house, as had I. He is the King of Kashi, the King of the Dead.

I stay mostly silent, taking refuge in the loss of words. It is not that I cannot speak. It is that once I start to speak, people will ask me questions, they will want to know. They will ask me my name. And speaking my name will make my loss complete. If I protect my name and my story with my silence, my parents will still be alive, my village will still be there. And I will be married.

Of late I dream of my husband. Even though we never lived together and I did not know him, he is… was… still my husband, partner of my destiny. I construct and deconstruct his face a thousand times. Sometimes, I wander outside and sit on the sand and use my fingers to draw his face. I never get it right.

Frustrated, I hit my head with my hands over and over again. As if by doing so my brain will connect with my hands and let me draw my own destiny. Yet I know it is of no use. My destiny is predetermined, as was his. Somewhere in the river he floats, food for the fish, drifting, putrefying and utterly dead.

'She is hitting her head again.' I hear the voices of my rescuers descend around me.

'Quick! Help me get her inside. Poor, poor mad thing.' A mixture of pity, fear and revulsion is in that voice. I dared not open my eyes for fear that they, the instruments of my sight, would swim away from me, leaving me blind and even more helpless. I am not mad. It is only that I know, see and feel things that others cannot.

I speak only to ask for food and water. I use my thoughts to try and exorcize my memories of the past, and of my name and of the life that was taken away from me. The rest of the time I devote to the story I write upon my skin.

I have made my body a battlefield of scars on which is being born my own saga, my epic. Some scars the river gave me. Others I create myself. I use any sharp thing I can find. I search for dark and lonely corners and mark myself in places on my body others cannot see.

Into my inner thigh I carve the name I cannot say aloud. My name. I clutch a jagged stone firmly and press its edge against my tender skin. With a little more pressure the skin parts and in that instant, the pain washes over me. It throbs like a reminder of life, giving me a message of reassurance. I am not dead. Blood oozes out in a thin red trickle and I smear it around until my skin glows pink and alive. Then, tenderly, I wipe it away. As if by caring for myself like a mother, my pain will melt. It does, for a moment, then engulfs me again. I look for a hidden, unblemished place on my body, which is a difficult task. Even my scars have scars. I write my own story upon myself in a language only I can understand.

Some nights I sense someone watching over me. Just to see me, to check if I breathe, to ascertain I am alive. I feel a presence but cannot identify it. I know it is a man. I will find out who he is. His presence comforts me. I drift away in a slow-flowing dream. I feel the texture of his dry fingertips as they lightly touch the skin of my face and gradually he becomes familiar to me. I feel as if he has always been an unspoken part of me, a link in my destiny. I sigh deeply as sleep overcomes me.

~

I sleep on a string cot in a little room that is used to store grain. I am comforted by the musty, dusty smell of the wheat and rice and lentils. Strangely it reminds me of home, of the little granary where the bounty from my father's field was stored.

It is only when I fall asleep that the nightmare returns. As I shift in my sleep trying to escape the giant, wet tendrils of the water hyacinth, I come awake. Then I feel him, that unseen presence, beside my string cot. In the dark I can see only the whites of his eyes and that of his clothes. He is closer to me now than he has ever been. I turn to him.

'Shhhh,' he whispers.

'I know you.' My voice trembles.

'How do you feel now? Do you remember your name?'

'I remember everything. I do not want to say my name,' I respond as if ordered to speak.

'You are safe, River Girl. No harm shall come to you in my house.'

'You are…' I sit up to try and get a better look at him. Now I am fully awake, fully aware.

He laughs, 'The most powerful and the most feared and hated man in Kashi.' His tone is bitter yet proud.

'The King of the Dead,' I whisper.

He laughs again as he comes closer. I feel the heat of his body as he sits on the cot beside me. I reach out and trace his face with my hands. I feel as if I have been waiting aeons to touch him, to make him real, to feel him. His face is older than the one I should have drawn on the sand, that of my dead husband. Somewhere between imagining my husband's face and the lines in the sand, the Dom Raja's features had conquered my intent and my desire. I realize that this nose, those eyes, that mouth, leaning over me have haunted me day and night since my arrival in Kashi. This was the face that my fingers had felt compelled to draw over and over again in the sand.

I draw his portrait now every day, more distinctly than I had before, though I have never seen him in the daylight. Into the damp sand I furrow every nook and cranny of his face. The hooded, deep-set, small eyes. The strong widow's peak from which his hair springs back with vitality. The wide mouth with its thick lips and slightly protruding teeth. I have felt his grainy skin, pitted with pockmarks from an early bout with smallpox.

'I know you,' I whisper to the face in the sand.

'Why do people fear and despise you?' I ask him in the night.

'Because I do what they cannot. I am there, with their dead ones when they can bear to be there no longer. When they cannot see the fat splutter in the fire, the head crack open, the skin burn away. They need me and they hate me.'

'Why do you keep me here?' I ask.

I feel the smile in his voice as he kisses my forehead. 'Where would you go?'

'I am not mad,' I say. He has not called me that but the word hangs heavily in the air. Where would you go, mad girl?

'Madness is the best weapon you have in this world, River Girl.' His voice hypnotizes me.

'I like that name. River… Nadee. I think I will keep it.' And I do.

I call myself Nadee, the river, and give myself to him completely.

~

I grow stronger each day, or at least my body does. My wild eyes and tangled hair and scattered speech during the day still make people call me mad. Sometimes an old woman, who is assigned to keep an eye on me, sees the blood trickling from a hidden cut and clucks her tongue in annoyance. No one knows where the blood comes from. They do not understand that I do it myself. They do not care enough to ask, nor I to tell them.

I walk along the side of the river now, every day, searching for my life. I sit on the edge of the bank and look for it carefully, slowly, my hands moving unceasingly as they swirl through the water. A man stops me once, hand heavy on my arm.

'What are you doing?' he asks. His words are innocuous but I can see the lust in his eyes as he examines me.

'I am looking for my life. Have you seen it?' I squint up at him from where I squat. The sun shines behind his head blanking his face into a silhouette.

He backs away. 'They let mad people come here now?' he shouts to no one in particular. He leaves.

I sit on the stone ghats and scoop up the water with my cupped hands. I find nothing. The sunlight glints through the holy liquid as I let it flow past my fingers back into the river. Even though I know that my life is already set on its predetermined path, I yearn to find it. The river took it away from me. The river is where I shall find it.

Moments of lucidity creep up on me, unaware, at night. Is it because that's when you visit me, King of the Dead? I wonder.

'Tell me what you do?' I trace the corded sinews of his arms as he lies beside me.

'I burn the dead. I take their sins upon my soul. The living make me rich so I can help the dead go to heaven. To be free from the circle of life.'

'I want to be free,' I whisper into his mouth. When we are together I forget everything for a while. I cannot tell how long we have been like this. When did his visits of concern and curiosity become this? I do not know, or care.

In the stillness of the night, he tells me. 'You are free. Others are free because of wealth or through the strength of their bodies. But your mind is free.'

'They call me mad,' I complain to him.

'You feel things they fear. You know things you should not.' He comforts me, steals away my loneliness for an instant.

Morning returns and I am alone again. I hide myself in a corner and sit back on my thigh to plump it out. Yesterday I found a treasure: a small, sharp knife that is used to cut through rough sacks in the granary. I have kept it for myself. Lovingly I carve into the skin of my thigh. Then I cut horizontally into one of the folds on the inside of my wrist, following the natural line. I am not trying to kill myself. I never cut deep enough to kill. I just want to know that I can. If I need to. Some day. Today I just want to ease the pain. To feel it spurt out of me, emerge from deep within me and free me from its grip, even if it is just for an instant.

'What are you doing?' my old woman protector asks, horrified. She snatches the knife away. I do not have the energy to resist.

'Cutting helps me,' I look at her, annoyed at the interruption.

'You are quite mad. Crazy!' She returns outside. This is none of her business. This is not what she is paid to do. I think she has given up on me and I am glad.

She comes to me later as I lie asleep, upon his portrait in the sand, by the river. She has a comb with her and some perfumed oil. Silently she nudges me awake. First she pours some of the copper-coloured oil into one palm, rubbing her hands together to warm it. Then she laces my scalp and hair with it. The comb navigates its way through the now slippery tangles. Some knots she can't untangle. They break off in her hands and she rolls them into balls. Soon she has a large tangled ball of my hair by her side. My scalp aches from her pulling and tugging.

She braids my hair tightly, pulling the skin of my forehead taut.

'There,' she says, as if trying to make amends for some imagined wrong.

'What is your name?' I ask. 'I don't even know your name.'

She uses her oil-slick hand to adjust the sari over her head which is shaved bald.

'Rajni. You can call me Rajni Tai,' she says.

'I like it.' I smile, then ask, 'Rajni Tai?'

'Yes?' she responds with a question of her own.

'Why is your head shaved?'

She seems stunned, as if I had clutched her hand and brought her out of the dark squinting in the merciless light of the day. 'Because I am a widow,' she answers. 'I was married for less than a day when my husband was killed by his enemies. I was eleven then. I have lost count of how old I am now.'

'Why are you here?'

'Enough,' she put up her hands. 'I was told to look after you.I have no choice for I have to do what he tells me to do. I owe him and his family too much. Yes, I feel sorry for you sometimes, sorry because you are mad. But I do not have to answer your questions.' She leaves, her eyes fixed on the sand.

I realize that I too am a widow. True, I had not seen my husband since we were children, never set foot in his house. But in the eyes of God and man I had been married and now I was a widow.

Gingerly I remove the gold stud from my nose. I wrap it in the stained pink silk of my sari along with a few strands of blue and gold I pull out from the peacock feather, and tuck it close to my heart. I run my hands over the oily surface of my neatly braided hair. I need to cut it close to my scalp, like Rajni Tai. I have no knife any more, nothing sharp to transform myself into the widow I am.

I find a stone. It is tapered on one side and its edges are jagged and serrated. I start sawing at my hair. I expect the hair to fall cleanly away but the stone is too blunt. All I manage to do is nick my scalp, rubbing it raw.

Streams of blood blind my eyes, flowing into them. Some flow down my face and fall… drop, drop, drop into the waters of the river. I wonder fleetingly if they will wash over the remains of my home. Pain finally penetrates into my consciousness. Rajni Tai comes back later and leads me away in resigned silence

That night the King of the Dead feels my bandaged head.

'Why?' he asks.

'I think I too am a widow,' I whisper back.

'Shhhh… don't think about such things. Don't say them.' His voice resonates inside my head. I know he has given me permission to lie, to say I was never married, never widowed. 'All right,' I whisper to him. I believe him. I don't know why but I do. I whisper something else that is torn with pain from the depths of me, something I don't want to say but am compelled to. 'What?' he strains to hear me.

'Do you know?' I ask. My voice trails away.

'Know what?' he asks.

'Do you know that I already know that I will kill you one day?' I drift into a hazy sleep, feeling his arms tighten around me.

3

Ganga: River of Stories

They call me Mother Goddess, patient and loving. My devotees believe I wash away their sins. They do not truly know me, as I am, who I am, my truths and my realities. I am the river of stories. These stories swim within me, swirling inside and between my liquid coils. I whisper them to those who listen, to those who can hear the silences nestled between the lapping of my waves. I have so many tales. Where should I begin? Perhaps you want to hear about my descent to earth. Yes, most people are fascinated with that one.

Once I flowed unfettered in the heavens, a beautiful and desirable goddess, out of reach of man, utterly unattainable. Then Bhagirath, a mortal, looking to atone for the immeasurably evil sins of his ancestors, persuaded me to come down to the earth and wash over their ashes, thus enabling their trapped souls to break free from an ancient curse and enter heaven freely. I was the only one who had the power to dissolve the weight of the sins that torment human souls, setting them eternally free. I said yes. I still berate myself every day for agreeing to his prayerful pleas. For, while the nightmarish existence of Bhagirath's ancestors, caught between the worlds, ended, my nightmare began. I have been trapped on earth for an eternity.

I still do not know why I allowed myself to be swayed by his words of praise. He appealed to my greatness and my powers and

I was susceptible to his flattery. That weakness is my one flaw and I have suffered greatly for it. Even after I agreed to his request, a dilemma remained.

The force of my cascade from heaven would surely destroy the earth and shift it from its axis. Bhagirath then propitiated Lord Shiva who offered to break my fall. Lord Shiva, the all-powerful who wears garlands of snakes around his neck, his senses enhanced by the drugged smoke he inhales. Lord Shiva, the destroyer of the universe, who holds the world in its delicate balance, poised eternally between the powers of creation and the seductions of humanity. He is spectacular, a fitting mate for me. I had always coveted him, lusted for him, wanted to be near him, become one with him and merge with his essence. I would get him in exchange for what I had to do.

But he was married to Parvati. I was naïve, even stupid perhaps. I thought he would become captivated with me once he saw me, once I flowed into his being, once we touched and were made one. I was certainly more beautiful, more lyrical and more graceful than Parvati. I had heard she had a quick, explosive temper, whereas I was known for my calm, serene beauty and a temper that took ages to simmer and seethe. Surely I could tempt him away from her. I am a shimmering, luminous seductress and beneath my calm surface I churned with desire for the dark lord. What a pair we would make: Shiva, that most dynamic and mysterious of gods, the ultimate sensualist, and Ganga, the most holy and revered of rivers. I was sure I would succeed. Certain that I would make him mine forever. I was determined to make him forget Parvati. Together he and I could rule the worlds.

So I flowed into his matted locks and he smiled in his lazy, disinterested manner, ignoring me and all my attributes. Even as I saturated his hair, even as I flowed down his forehead and into his half-closed eyes, he remained lost, as always, submerged in the thoughts of his soulmate, his Parvati, and I knew I had left my home for nothing. I tumbled playfully down his body but he remained untouched. Shiva paid no attention to my wiles, to the feel of my malleable body on his. For his mind, his body and his soul were filled with her, his evil-tempered consort. He loved her in ways that never die. Through the ages, she was born, always mortal, always fated to die and be reborn. Each time he lost her to death he continued to love her. He waited, for he knew she would return to him. Always. In all her forms. And she did. She returned to him in many guises and he always recognized her and made her his own, again and again. I could not compete with her, with this. His passionate love for her, his hunger for her untransformed soul rendered all others invisible, even me.

I was gathered into his matted hair, trapped, feeling his pulsing, tangible power and the icy chill of his indifference. I felt tired and defeated. I longed to return, to go back to my beautiful home. How could I? There was no way back for me. I could never return. Would never return. He let his hair down, his drenched locks reaching past his knees. It was already too late.

I was freed and I descended upon the earth. I made the land green where I flowed through, filling fields with my bounty. And I washed away the sins of those who bathed in me.

Bhagirath's ancestors entered heaven. Lord Shiva was hailed as a friend of mankind once again. And songs were composed in my glory. They call me Ganga Ma: Ganga the Mother, the redeemer of sin, the heavenly river.

Generations have passed. I have received nothing for my act of sacrifice, nothing except empty praises and the company of the dead. My calm serenity is periodically consumed by long periods of slow-simmering and terrible rage. Sometimes I get so angry I can barely control myself. I avenge my trapped existence by claiming portions of the earth, destroying land and fields, houses and people, gathering them all into my watery embrace. I do this until I am sated. Then I pull back and I am content, for a while.

~

I whisper this and many other secrets to the girl who carries a strange burden that she struggles to understand. Lover of the Dom Raja by night, she is a mad seeker by day. She visits me every day and I tell her stories. It is the least I can do. I give her stories in exchange for her life. That I cannot return, for even I lack the power to reverse time and fate. I realize what I have done to her and the knowledge lies uneasily within me.

I remember her whispered confidences, her fears and hopes and joys from another time. I recall that once she sat by my side in another place and told me her secrets. Like many others do. Still, she was different somehow. She would tell me things that were yet to happen. She could sense my building rage, see the fury I was about to unleash and it filled her with terror. She tried to divert me, tried to reason with me, to plead, but to no avail for I was deaf to her.

I can tell, despite her air of sad detachment that she is curious about the songs she hears from Meera Ghat. She listens intently to the hymns praising the gods, dozens of voices praying for an early death. She listens as if the lyrics and the singers are telling her something that she needs to remember. I try to help by telling her about Meera Ghat and its inhabitants.

Meera is the ghat, the shore lined by dozens of eroding stone steps, for widows who journey to Kashi to die. It does not matter if they are eight or eighty; death is the only goal to which they can aspire, the only desire they dare utter out aloud.

They sing hymns to Lord Krishna, lover and seducer of thousands. Krishna, the vagabond flirt whose heart remained forever true to only one woman, Radha, his eternal lover. When Radha was with him, all others receded into the shadows. Like Meera. Poor Meera! She was forever an afterthought. She meant nothing to him. She appeared no different to him than any others from his legion of devotees. But for Meera, Krishna was the unrivalled object of her devotion and boundless love.

Meera was a desert princess, who as a child had vowed to become one with the dusky god who enchanted her with music from his magic flute. She felt the power of his divine presence reach to her through the stone statue that her family had worshipped for centuries. He became real to her and she was his from that moment on.

She knew him as a deity, an entity, a force and yet she could look past all the intangibles and see him. And love him. She was married off to a prince but she still sought Krishna everywhere, in everything. She composed songs, pouring out her longing for her mystical lover in every word. These same hymns, years after her death, now echo at the ghat that is named for her. It exemplifies the purity of her doomed, unrequited love and devotion.

At the top of the steps of the ghat, crumbling at my shores stands a simple white building, blackened with age. This is where they live, the widows of Kashi, the denizens of Meera Ghat. The mad girl wants to know more about Meera. She begs me to tell her more, to fill her head with thoughts of Meera so that she can be liberated from her own emotions, if only for a moment. So I continue.

Meera's husband, enraged and jealous, feeling a cuckold, tried to kill her many times, but she was always saved by Lord Krishna. It was Krishna who turned poison into nectar and blessed her with his presence, pleased with her devotion to him. Meera, the wandering mendicant who was born a princess, died on the streets, penniless and consumed by her love. Meera the devoted, Meera, mad with love for her Krishna, sings,

So deep is this attachment
That Meera is maddened by it.
I sing his praises in all the
Alleys and bylanes.
I was born in a palace
Now I am simply a mad devotee.
People say, Meera, the princess
Is mad.

The women of Meera Ghat are white ghosts. I see them each day at sunrise and at dusk. Bald heads covered, young and old, eyes downcast, they walk into me, their bodies parting the gentle waves, their lips moving ceaselessly in prayer. Like Meera, they pray to their Lord and ask him to deliver their souls in his presence. They beseech him to love them a little. He is their only refuge in a world that scorns them.

I tell the burdened one about one such widow. She was young, and beautiful despite her shaved head, and was at the time my story begins at the height of her youth. She was widowed when she had been a bride for barely a day, her husband killed by his enemies because of a property dispute. And she was sent to Meera Ghat to live out the rest of her days. She tried so very hard to fit in, to do as she was told. She ate one meal a day, always before sunset, no spices, and no strong-smelling vegetables, nothing that would make the food palatable. She was a walking wound, her body and soul hungry for love.

The man she fell in love with was a priest who led the widows in prayer every morning. He was young, his romantic soul filled with poetry, and he was entranced by her large, soulful eyes. As he handed her flowers for prayer, his fingers would fleetingly caress hers. A tingle would run all through her and she lived as if within a fever. Sometimes hot, then cold, shivering deliciously at the very thought of him. She could not bear to be away from his presence.

They ran away together. For one month they lived as man and wife, in a little village. Her hair grew out in soft waves. He loved running his hands through it. Then they were caught and brought back by the establishment of priests who run Kashi and enforce the laws of morality. And he, the love of her life, more familiar to her than the husband who had died the day they were wed, betrayed her.

He said she had deliberately enticed him. That she seduced him. The weakness of his flesh was blamed on her evil female spell. She was a wicked woman and he was a mere man, bewitched by her beguiling eyes and the promises she made with her sinful body.

He was sent to another temple away from her temptations. She was publicly humiliated, her face blackened, her head shaved again, paraded through the streets of the city as an example to all who dared challenge the ancient mores. Then the Dom Raja, the grandfather of Nadee's lover, had intervened. He was able to do this because he was feared, reviled and powerful and none dare defy him. She became part of his household, a servant, bound to the compound by chains of gratitude and duty. No one knows why he saved her, why he gave her safe haven, though they all talked of the possible reasons. For the first time in his life the Dom Raja came up against someone more betrayed by their birth and destiny than he. Or perhaps it was because she was a beautiful woman and a Brahmin widow. And he was an untouchable man despite all his power and wealth. Perhaps through her body he could exorcize the demons of his birth for a little while. Or perhaps this is all conjecture. Perhaps even I, Mother Goddess, do not know what truly lives in men's hearts and makes them act the way they do.

~

I tell the mad girl about her King of the Dead. He has lost count of the generations that made him who he is. He learned from his father and grandfather the intricate rituals of death. How high to build the pyre. How much sandalwood and how much ghee would be needed for fully destroying the flesh. He knew them all. He knew how long a body needs to burn, and at what temperature, to be completely incinerated. He knew how many priests are to be fed to guarantee safe passage for the soul on its upward journey. People ask him these and other questions and he always knows the answers.

He has guided countless first-born sons on the proper technique of cracking the skulls of their dead parents, thus releasing the soul from the bonds of flesh. And he has learned to escort the family away, before the body crackles and twists in the fire, rising upright and becoming a burning ghoulish sceptre. Who wants that as the final memory of their dead mother? I chuckle at the macabre thought.

The Dom Raja took their money and learned to bear their revulsion and fear. He craved respect, not fear, but that was the one thing in Kashi he could not buy. He could not buy his way out of his destiny. He knew Kashi needed him while despising him for that need.

So he built the walls of his house higher, shielding himself from the outside. At his gate he placed two giant stone tigers, poised to attack, proclaiming his supreme position in the city. He amassed his fortune and learned to squander it on prostitutes and courtesans. Money poured into and out of his compound like water. Death is a lucrative business. He has little of himself left to give the mad River Girl. I take some pleasure in telling her that, trying to jolt her out of her calm, trying to make her save herself from destruction.

'He visits you only at night,' I say, 'when he has wearied of the practiced wiles of prostitutes.'

She listens silently.

'But even they get a string of flowers, a jewel, some money. What does he give you, mad girl, Nadee?'

I do not tell her that sometimes the tears that run down his cheek are not just caused by the strong, acrid smoke from the pyres. In the dark he directs his army of death attendants. The bodies burn day and night for death does not respect time. He tells his servants how best to stoke the fires. He makes sure that all body parts are fully engulfed in the flames. Sometimes if a family is too poor to buy enough wood to reduce the body to ash, he commands his servants to toss the half-burned body into my bosom. The business of death has to remain profitable.

Knowledge translates to power. Besides it is such a small thing, this information I withhold. No one can begrudge me that. Sometimes I feel that is all the power I have left. Besides I am doing her a favour by not telling her all.

Her voice from the past percolates into my consciousness, mingling with her scattered speech in the present, and I understand that her burden lies heavily within her. I know that she cannot fully grasp its place in her life. I know she mourns her family still. But she will get over it. She talks to me. She tells me how much she hates me for taking everything away from her. But she is compelled to come to me because I am her last link with her life. She looks for her life within my waters, always coming up empty. I confess there are times I feel sorry for her. She is mad and alone.

~

I try to distract her with stories for I want her to stop what she is about to do. 'I know I shall kill him. I don't know why, but I know I shall,' the mad girl says to me.

'Perhaps because he molests you. Because you get the leavings of prostitutes,' I venture to guess, trying to fill her head with my thoughts.

'No, no. It is not that. I was ready. He means something to me, to my life. There was no force.' She says the words, but I know she thinks about what I tell her. She lets my words run through the folds of her mind and pool into dark thoughts that I cannot fully decipher.

'Then what is it?' I ask.

'I wish I knew,' she says slowly.

I know she wants to leave Kashi to avoid this thing she must do. But what is predetermined pulls her back, keeping her where she is. We are not so unlike, this mad girl and I. We are both trapped and angry. Both bound by a destiny we cannot escape. They call me Mother Goddess. She calls herself Nadee.

4

Redemption

The river whispers maddening things to me in a slow, sinuous rhythm that wraps itself around me until I am forced to pretend I am deaf, that I cannot hear her. Over and over again she speaks softly to me, never leaving me alone, never letting me draw a breath, never giving me time to think. She continues, drawing me closer and closer to the brink of complete madness. She does not know it, no one really knows it, but there is a part of me that is still trying to hang on to a tenuous strand of sanity, a part that wants to hold on to something other than the darkness that threatens to consume me. On the razor-sharp edge balanced between sanity and madness, I try to exist without giving in, try to survive without breaking and scattering apart.

Her whispers are doing their best to make me sever my bond with what is real, to make me skitter off the narrow edge and plunge into an abyss from which there will be no escape, in which I will drown and never find myself or my life. I am powerless in her grasp. The way she speaks to me. The strange, inexplicable way she makes me talk to her. I try to stay away from her but I cannot. She is sneaky, so insidious, so… so evil, that sometimes I cannot distinguish between my voice and hers, my thoughts and hers. She makes me wonder, where does she end and I begin?

Her voice burrows within me, flowing inside me. 'Nadee…' she says, in a fluent, gentle cadence, 'there is only one way out of this trap. Let go. Your family is dead.' Her words rush into each other, colliding and bursting like bubbles in the air before slithering into my ears, filling my mind until they crowd out every other thought, leaving me at her mercy. Others are oblivious to her insidious, hissing, sibilance and go about their business. I want to scream at them, to take them by the shoulders and say, 'Listen to me. Shhhh… be quiet. Can't you hear her? Can't you? She is trying to make me do things, evil mad things. Help me. Stop her.' But there is no one who I have the right to ask for help, no one bound to me with threads of love and blood. No one who is mine.

I welcome the rough arms of my lover at night and I know now, clearly, who he is. I also remember who I am and what I must do. My lover has a wife and many children, some as old as I am. I hear them at the other end of the compound, shielded from my newly-curious eyes by a wall that is twice my height. They laugh and talk as they run and play, the older ones taking care of their younger siblings, whose giggles and bubbling happiness eat into my consciousness like a worm tunnelling its way into a rose. The knowledge of their place in his life brushes against the edges of my carefully built cocoon and chills my skin with a blast of reality.

'What do you tell her, about me?' I ask him. The intervening days have made me curious about his wife, the woman who shares his name, his life, his children and his destiny. I am always outside his world. There is no place in his life – his real life, for me.

He laughs. 'Why does she need to know about you?'

I am silent for I have no answer, only a rising, unfamiliar rage that threatens to swamp me. So I persist.

'Does she know about me?' I ask the question slowly, demanding an answer.

'She knows that a mad girl, a victim of circumstance, was fished out of the river and that the household… my household… gives her shelter. That is all she needs to know. This is my house, after all.' His voice is strong and matter of fact and it commands me to ask no more. He has told me all I need to understand. He has told me I am unimportant, that I barely exist except for his need for me. I am not me. I am just his. I became his, for his convenience, when he gave me refuge.

I am silenced, though thoughts still race around in my head, dashing themselves behind my eyes, forcing me to listen. And Ganga laughs silently at my confusion while feeding me maddening possibilities. She enters my consciousness trying to leach me of sentient thought, of the power to make decisions. This realization races through me with a sudden speed. I gather the tattered cloak of my resolve around me. I am ready.

~

I feel his rough fingertips trace the tiny scars on my body, his raspy yet tender touch on the scabbed lines at the place where my hair meets my forehead. One by one he kisses the healing wounds, and for an instant all questions and fears and doubts melt away inside me. I know he has told me I have no rights upon him and I know that he is correct. Still some hidden, dark impulse claws to life within me.

I drift through his household every day as if I am invisible. I live in his granary, eat his food and bathe in the river at dawn. I hear the sounds of his other life through the dividing wall between his home and the rest of the compound. I hear the shrieks of laughter and cries and I hear his wife – at least I think she is his wife – calling to her, to their children. Her voice burrows inside my head like a malevolent spirit until I cannot escape her presence, her existence, her life and her power. His other life becomes real and battles against the trance-like state of our furtive meetings. I find myself more and more drawn to Ganga's taunting suggestions.

~

Today I have made a discovery; found a new treasure to replace the one taken away by Rajni Tai. I now no longer need sharp rocks and jagged pieces of discarded metal, for in the refuge of my granary I have found a scythe, left behind by some careless worker. It is curved like the quarter moon, sharp like the edge of my reality and as precious as the life I seek. It glows like well-worn silver and is warmed by the heat of my body as I enfold it within my palm. When I press it upon myself, it parts my skin like the whispered kiss of a familiar lover.

I try to spot the Dom Raja during the day and can never see him. Does he hide from me? Or does he look so much like the countless others that go in and out of his house that I do not know him? Do I recognize him only in the dark, as if his presence were an obscenely secret blight, a shameful thing? I know his face like my own. I have drawn it upon the sand a thousand times but I struggle to recognize it in flesh and blood. The bright light of day makes him a stranger to me. Men of all ages and types come and go from this compound at all times of the day and night and my eyes skitter between them, trying to translate the memory of his touch into the concrete reality of his presence.

~

A path from the compound leads to the main burning grounds a few miles away. Sometimes when the wind blows in the right direction I can smell the smoke and feel its whispery, grey breath wreathe itself around me like warm gauze, muffling my senses. It drifts over the river in a haze and carries within its fragility the smells of burning hair and roasting flesh.

Tonight I shall go to him. I shall take back the power that he has taken from me when he comes to me and leaves as he pleases. Now as I begin to emerge from a place deep within myself, I know where I will find him because each night in his arms I have smelled the aroma of death in every pore of his flesh.

I spend the day by the river listening to Ganga's soft sounds, her muttering whispers. As the sun dips below the horizon, sunlight dissolves within her waters, turning it the colour of gold tinged with blood. It is time.

Most of the men who work the night shift have left the compound through the back door. I wait until I cannot hear their voices any more. The home – his home – on the other side of the wall is still and silent. The children must be in bed, their mother asleep. I walk through the gate and on to the well-packed earthen path leading to the place where the Dom Raja rules the night.

I enter the portals of hell. The red glow from hundreds of fires lights up the sky in a nightmare-scape. Embers fly like angry red fireflies, turning grey as they fall to the ground, their fury and heat expended into powdery ashes. The men stoke the fires, regulating their temperature, pouring ghee on faltering flames. From one of the pyres I see a dangling arm fall out and touch the ground. The fingers are extended and stiff and a single, cracked, green, glass bangle on the wrist winks in the artificially ruddy day. Dirt is encrusted into each line of the palm that faces me as I walk towards it. One of the attendants shoves the arm back into the flames efficiently.

Night is when the dead rule, forcing the living to tend to them. As men, women and children burn, engulfed in purifying fire, their bodies render their fat, making the flames dance in sudden spurts of energy. Bones crack like cannon shots, sounding from every direction, strange staccato background music to the jokes and songs being bandied about by the attendants of death.

'Oof, my back hurts after lifting that one on to the fire,' complains one.

'Aaah, that's what it was. I thought you were celebrating your wedding night with that fat one.' The speaker laughs at his joke and the others join in.

'You sister-fucker! At least I pick the women. We all know what you do with the men.' The victim of the original joke spits on the ground in triumph as he makes an obscene gesture.

As they see me approach silence descends. I search their black-stained, sweaty faces, their reddened eyes and callous expressions.

I see him directing one of his men to build a new pyre. He is the only one there still wearing his shirt, though it is streaked with soot. In the night, in the flickering light from the fires, his face is familiar and instantly recognizable. I know him.

He turns to face me, a long line of black soot running from his forehead to the edge of his lips, dividing his face in two. It is the first time I have clearly seen his face, outside of my mind, illuminated as it is by the red flames and the blue, smoky, ghost light around us. It is as I had always drawn it. Broad and fleshy, the skin is rough, dark leather, the little dips of the pockmarks making symmetrical lines, the moustache, black thick wires, springing from his upper lip. His eyes are red because of the smoke and the heat of the flames that dance around us.

'You should not be here… cannot be here,' he says to me.

'Why? I wanted to see you. To come and see you,' I enunciate each word clearly, emphasizing my control, proclaiming my power over my faculties.

'It is bad luck for you to be here.'

'Why?'

'So many reasons. You are a woman. And,' he pauses, 'you are a widow.'

I hear the crackle of wood and bones and the muted whispers of his men as they go about their chores. I cannot speak. His words echo and re-echo inside me, making me mute.

'Come,' he says kindly, 'I will take you home.'

'So you can come to me in the night and leave before daybreak like always?' I ask belligerently, standing my ground, letting Ganga's voice swim in my head, letting my emotions plunge towards a dangerous whirlpool. I cannot stop what I am feeling, what I must do, even if I wanted to. I give in. He grasps my hand and forces me to walk away from the presence of his silent men. As if in a trance I comply, listening to his voice, trying to understand his message.

'You never complained. You invited me. I saved you and protected you. I would never do anything to harm you, against your will, I swear it.' His words ring with truth and I fall silent for I cannot put into words the tearing emotions that roil around inside me and demand release.

We arrive back at my little room and I inhale the dusty scent of the stored wheat and millet. It is true, he has never taken what was not offered and never did anything against my will, but I am angry. I feel my rage like a river of blood gurgling and rushing in my ears, pushing aside calm thoughts, drowning my resistance to what I know I am about to do. I don't even know if I am angry with him, with Ganga or with myself. All I feel is this beast within me that threatens to consume me unless I control it as it roars inside my head like an enraged, wounded lion. I watch his face as he speaks and the sound of his words seems to come from a distance, somewhere other than from his moving lips. Somewhere away from me.

He is a man, he says, a weak man tormented by many demons. The demons of his lust, the circumstances of his birth, his inescapable profession and the dry despair of his life have all conspired to drive him towards me, to seek something in me while reaching for feelings and compulsions within him. I was brought to him, borne in the arms of the river goddess, like a gift, and he had felt something, an emotion. That emotion had been the flaw in his grandfather and father's makeup and he had not escaped its legacy.

'I wanted to protect you. For once, there was someone more wretched, more in need of humanity than I. And I could not help myself. I could have sent you to Meera Ghat or somewhere else, a temple perhaps. But I had to… had to have you. To save you and to save myself. And I helped you. You know I did. I gave… gave you shelter and food and… love,' his voice dropped to a whisper and then died away. 'While you remain here with me I will know that I am a person of some real value, a man worthy of something more than just fear and hatred and greed for my wealth. If you go away, that man within me dies. And that… that I cannot let happen.'

I understood. He saw in me – a battered, exhausted, sad, self-mutilator – a chance at redemption. I was his chance of saving his own soul from the demonic flames of his life's work and the hell that awaited him outside the realm of this world. I was his good deed as Rajni Tai had been his grandfather's. Just as his grandfather had saved Rajni to keep her around as a reminder of his generosity of spirit, so had he kept me close to him, as a living embodiment of his ultimate humanity. I was not Nadee to him. I was an indescribable, intangible thing without feelings or emotions or form. I was not a person. I was just a means, a vehicle to cleanse his spirit and soul. Not a woman. 'I… am… not… your… redemption,' I say through chattering teeth. I am chilled as if the swirling coils of the river were lapping against my skin on a cold, cold night.

'Yes, yes you are. And as long as you are with me, my soul is safe. I will know that I have done at least one good thing. And I will know that my sins will be redeemed in the next life and that knowledge will keep me going… it is what keeps me going. It will not let me give up when these thoughts, these feelings, these fears threaten to devour me.' His voice quivers with the fear of impending loss. It is the first time that I have seen him not in complete control, the only time when he seems to ask… to beg me for something.

'I cannot stay here anymore,' I say resolutely. I know where I have to go and I cannot let him stop me. I am struggling, trying still, even now, at this moment, to not let my dreadful foreknowledge rule my life.

He senses a change in me. I am different somehow and his voice stalls as he tries to re-assert his power over me.

'No, you cannot go. I won't let you leave. You will not leave.' The face I have imagined and drawn a thousand times creases with anger and fear. I have no doubt of his power; his status, reviled though he was, towered over all the priests and merchants of the city. This is the City of the Dead and he is its King. I cannot leave if he will not let me. I cannot battle him within his territory. I falter.

'You know I will not let you leave. Come now. Forget all this foolishness.' A laugh accompanies his words. A laugh that echoes and is magnified inside my head, pushing aside everything else until I cannot bear its harsh reverberations as it hangs heavily in the air, mocking me and reminding me of my powerlessness. It fills the air long after he stops laughing, the sound coming at me in waves of derision. When I plunge the curved, sharp edge of the scythe into his chest, his face registers shocked surprise but no pain. Mercifully the laughter dies away abruptly and his eyes lock into mine with a feverish intensity, as if asking me a question. His hands come up and grasp mine where they still hold the handle of my weapon.

'You cannot stop me. I have to leave and I will leave,' I say, as his warm blood pulses over our joined fingers, drenching them.

'Your soul is free now.' I caress his brow as the life begins to flow out of him softly, gently. His head lies in my lap and I rock him back and forth, as his spirit flees, as he is liberated from his birth, his life and his work. He is free from the torment of Kashi. Free from his despised duties. Free from the sins of his birth and from his fears of the next life, free from his quest for redemption. He is redeemed. He had been right. I am his redeemer.

I hear the rattle in his throat which sounds like the little drum of the local monkey-man. His eyes begin to fix and stare past me, as if he has finally found what he was looking for. I feel him jerk violently, his back arching, his throat convulsing before he begins to stiffen in my arms. I lay his head down on the hard floor and leave before his life fully fades away. I am free.

5

House of Culture

Agra, Winter, 1571

From my window, if I stand at the correct angle, I can see the red stone walls of the massive fort. In the smoky haze of early morning when barely warm air meets the night-cooled ground, the fort seems ephemeral, insubstantial and strangely fragile despite its massive size. Even now, fifteen years after the first buildings were erected, workmen still labour night and day adding to its huge, rambling proportions. I wonder what life is like behind those gargantuan walls that straddle the horizon, within those soaring minarets and cupolas that seem to pierce the sky. I have heard about those ornate palaces, those giant halls, those fabled, lush gardens and gushing fountains. I let my imagination drift, making things grander than grand, larger than scale and more spectacular than any fantasy.

I have escaped, forever, the clutches of Ganga, her maddening stories and violent suggestions. In Agra flows the more serene Yamuna. Silver where the Ganga is gold, the Yamuna is a modest river, less ostentatious and a lower-ranking goddess. She flows by the fort, which stands on her shores, built there for strategic advantage against enemy invaders. I am far enough away to catch only fleeting silver glimpses of her and I am glad, for here in this house I have a routine and a new beginning. I am afraid that if I sit by her shores and listen to her soft music I will discover the echoes of Ganga within her waters. I fear that she carries within her the distilled spirit of her haughty relative.

My room is small. To be exact, it is not really a room, more a little alcove curtained off, at the end of a long corridor, with a small gash of a window through which I watch the city at night. I sought out this house over a year ago since I had only one commodity to peddle, one piece of merchandise to exorcize the demons of my past. But one look at my marked and pitted body, fresh red scars curving over darker older ones, and Amma Jaan, as everyone called the head of this household, said that I would scare away more customers than attract. Perhaps Amma Jaan was moved by a rare moment of pity, for she could have cast me out. Instead she took me in. Perhaps my wild hair and scarred body and the bundle of pink silk I keep tucked at my breast also had something to do with this decision.

Every house can always take in an extra servant, someone to run errands and attend to the needs of its inhabitants. I became that extra person, that convenience for this household and those who dwell in it – the courtesans of the most famous and perhaps most important house in Agra, the centre of its cultural universe. In this house passion and longing are expressed in sensuously delicate poetry. The art of conversation, the elaborate rules of etiquette, the rituals of good manners are elevated to new heights within these four walls. I rarely see my employer, busy as she is in her responsibilities of running the best-known brothel in Agra. She has mujras to plan, new patrons to attract, quality to maintain, not to mention that she has to constantly scan the realm for new talent, for which she travels to distant places within the empire.

I sweep and clean and attend to the capricious needs of the bejewelled and pampered women who live in the house. Their days are large, empty slashes of time. They have little to occupy themselves except food and the rituals of beauty.

Each morning begins with a lavish breakfast. Fresh fruit of the season, ghee-drenched parathas eaten with mint-flavoured kababs and hot, sweet tea are some of the treats they enjoy. Foods that I have never tasted before. Sometimes during the winter months, I am sent to the early morning market to fetch nihari, that most spicy, delicious stew of bony oxtail, meat and gelatinous blobs of fat, to be sopped up with pillowy mounds of naan.

After breakfast the most important work of the day begins, always a never-ending source of amazement and wonder to me. Their beauty regimens are elaborate and take hours to complete and patience to endure. A paste of turmeric, sandalwood powder and rosewater, combined with other aromatic spices and herbs, is slowly massaged onto every part of their bodies. Gradually the mixture dries and sloughs off, taking with it the roughness of their skin, leaving a perfumed, satiny-soft expanse that could seduce the most hardened man.

Long, lustrous hair is drenched with oil infused with the fragrance of aromatic flowers. This warmed oil, golden in the sunlight, is massaged into their scalps, coating each strand, until the hair grows slippery, smooth and perfumed. The women emerge from their baths with their hair glossed to a brilliant sheen, and their bodies gleaming and scented, cool and inviting.

As evening approaches, the pace picks up. Their hair is braided with ropes of jasmine and small roses wound into the long strands. Then the jewellery goes on, piece by piece, transforming these already beautiful women into supreme objects of desire and seduction.

~

I sit spellbound on the floor by the bed which is decorated with thousands of red rose petals gleaming like spots of blood on the pristine white sheets.

She takes the teeka and aligns the strand of tiny seed pearls, setting it into the centre parting of her hair. The diamond crescent within the gold and pearl circle of the ornament rests neatly on her forehead, drawing attention to her magnificent eyes that flash with dark fire. She picks up her diamond and ruby ring and threads it through her nose from where it dangles, swinging slightly, enticing glances to her full red lips. Paisley-shaped enamel and diamond earrings dangle from her soft lobes, brushing against the junction of her neck and shoulders. The ruby and gold necklace around her neck glows with a muted fire, paling only against the brilliance of her face.

For a long moment she stares at her features in the mirror, then she lines her eyes with black belladonna, making them glow even more, enhancing their wiles. Her lips shine bright, moist and predatory in the light of the lamps and her skin is downy soft, unblemished and smooth. She makes a face at herself in the mirror before she turns to me. 'What do you think, you mad girl? Do I look ready?'

I can only nod mutely, mesmerized by Agra's most famous, most desired, most wondrous courtesan, Nafasat Bai. She laughs at my bemused reaction, but not unkindly. I spend more time taking care of her needs than of anyone else in the house for she is kind to me. She calls me mad often, but never with the bored viciousness of some of the other women, and she looks at me when she talks to me, not off to the side as if I am a speck of dust, a little bit of nothing.

She picks up her anklets. They are magnificent, thick ropes of gold adorned with thousands of tiny bells, exemplifying the most essential jewellery, as well as the chains that bind a courtesan to her life, forever outside the pale of society. The style of the anklet, its size, the number of its bells and the way it is worn, is what distinguishes a lady from a courtesan. A respectable woman wears anklets that are silent, modest and unassuming, drawing no attention to them or to her, in silver or in gold, if her family can afford it. They are like her, the honour of a household, and like honour they are circumspect and discreet. A courtesan's anklets, on the other hand, proclaim her profession aloud, in sounds that range from subtle flirtation to reckless, abandoned passion. And how the anklets are used distinguishes an amateur from a practiced seductress. But Nafasat Bai's anklets are more than mere anklets. They betray her electrifying presence well before she enters any room, they set the scene and whet the senses; they proclaim her superiority.

She is no longer a young woman, no longer even the most beautiful in the house. But when evening arrives and her anklets echo, enchanting and magical, she could fool anyone into believing she is the only woman who matters. Night is her realm and she, its glittering queen.

Nafasat Bai lives for the mujra, the evening of song, poetry and dance that compels the most powerful and the wealthiest men of the city to abandon their homes in favour of her presence. At night her skin glows like creamy silk shot with gold and her hair ripples and shines like restless night clouds through which the errant moonlight plays tricks.

She shakes out her anklets, jangling the bells, testing their sound, walking slowly, then fast, to check the cadence caused by her delicate stride. When she dances she moves slowly as if overcome by the languorous maladies of love and seduction, keeping time through the music of her anklets, making the accompanying musicians superfluous. As her feet lightly tap the ground in rhythm, the bells sound shy, flirtatious and elusive; when she stamps her feet they reflect her passionate fire.

But the rhythm of the anklets and even her fabled beauty and charm fade when compared to her voice. Her admirers have written paeans and odes to her voice, searching for words to describe its range and quality and pitch, and the feeling that throbs through its multi-layered, multi-textured surface, drawing her listeners into a spell from which there is no awakening. It is a voice found at the bottom of a goblet of the most potent wine, intoxicating, unsettling and dangerous. Her voice, it is said, could drive kings and saints insane, making them hapless captives, utterly in her power. In the streets of Agra, rumour had it that the empress kept the emperor away from this house through the use of black magic, so powerful was the magnetic pull of Nafasat Bai's voice.

I wonder about that sometimes. On still moonless nights, when stars hide their brilliance in the arms of dark clouds, when gossamer curtains billow outward as the wind enters houses stuffy with heat, when Nafasat Bai's throaty, husky, sad voice wafts through the air – does the emperor stop and listen? Does her peerless voice travel through the night, borne on the summer wind, breach the defenses of the fort and compel him to stop what he is doing? Does he sometimes look across the ramparts, across the dark roofs of his city and wonder at the source of this most hauntingly enticing sound?

~

Tonight she is as captivating as always. Her new lover is in attendance, a young nawab from a neighbouring town, newly wed and securely trapped within the silken skeins of her spell. He had seen and heard Nafasat Bai at his own wedding, where she had provided the entertainment. Even as he nodded a yes to the qazi's perfunctory questions, joining him in matrimony to a woman he had never met, his mind and heart were filled with the courtesan.

He had been married for thirty days now and had attended her mujra for twenty-eight evenings. From the first time they met their eyes had duelled in a game of mutual seduction. By his fifth visit he had convinced Nafasat Bai to give him access to her bed. Without a backward glance she had discarded her old lover and indulged in this new passion as if compelled by feelings that fall beyond the limits of reason, as if he – this young nawab – were the new architect of her fate. Her previous lover continues to attend her nightly mujras, but it is as though he has become invisible to her.

Her eyes glow, flash and flirt as she looks at her young nawab through down-swept lashes. Nawab Nawaz Ali Khan is at least a decade younger than Nafasat Bai. He is tall, with the slight build of a poet-dreamer. His hair falls in glistening curls to his shoulders and his blue-grey eyes pierce her soul.

She sings directly to him leaving no doubt in any who watch that her new lover and she are enthralled with each other. His eyes follow her every move, gliding over her body and face like caressing kisses. Between his fingers he restlessly crushes a garland of fragrant jasmine, as if trying to restrain himself, as if his fingers were on her skin, restless, hungry and eternally unsated.

The crystal chandeliers with their hundred candles, the snowy white sheets draped over padded long mattresses, adorned with ornate cushions for the patrons' comfort, the sparkling silver of the goblets and the deep garnet fire of the wine, create an atmosphere of languid poetry and lavish seduction.

Conversation between the assembled men and the courtesans evolves like an intricate dance. Flirtation so practiced it appears unforced, eyes that half close or open wide by turns, inviting deep looks and softly spoken wicked suggestions.

During this time, no courtesan can seem to deliberately favour one patron over another. Prominent families often sent their young sons to learn the rites and rituals of moving in high society. Their own mothers and sisters lived modest and secluded lives, burdened by housework, weddings and childbirth without any time to learn the art of conversation, the appreciation of poetry or the millions of little nuances that make people discerning and interesting. And their fathers were too busy with their own lives to educate their sons in these finer things in life which were after all the domain of the courtesan. The courtesans, especially in this house, were well educated; some were poets and those who were not had been taught an appreciation of poetry and the arts. Within this house of culture operating at the edge of society, the future courtiers and nobles of tomorrow were trained.

The crowd is always a mix of these young, callow students, over-eager and over-anxious, some young landowners and nawabs at the height of their own power, and several middle-aged and older men who have been attending mujras for years, for whom these evenings are both habit and tradition. Wine is poured into ornate goblets, conversation flows and the elaborate rituals unfold.

The delicate arching of a brow, the handing over of a paan wrapped in silver leaf and flavoured with lime paste, betel nuts, cardamom and clove, letting soft hands brush against someone just so, all of these are an art form. Promising the sweet torment of delayed gratification, it is all choreographed yet effortless and I am caught in the spell as surely as the patrons.

I watch every mujra from behind the curtains, running errands and trying to catch long glimpses of every move that Nafasat Bai makes, trying to mimic them. I pretend that she is looking into a mirror and I am her reflection. In her beautiful, unmarked body and smooth-skinned face I see perfection. Somewhere inside me I know that one day she and I will be very much alike, almost the same. We will become each other. As the sensation of knowing flows through and over me I feel old fears run through my veins like lightning.

As the evening draws to a close, the chandeliers are dimmed, acting as a polite signal for inebriated stragglers that the evening has ended and it is time to leave. Wine goblets lie scattered inside.

Crushed flowers dot the floor and the seating areas, filling the hall with a lilting perfume that mingles with the scents of desire and lust and commerce. I help clean up with some of the other servants, all of us sleepily rubbing our eyes. Amma Jaan wants all evidence of the night gone as soon as the hall has emptied.

I watch Nafasat Bai turn fluidly, one hip thrust out in a potent invitation. Her full skirt swishes around, continuing to swing even as she stops. She looks at him through her long lashes, her lips in a trembling pout. Her flower-bedecked braid lies over one shoulder, falling to a spot where it grazes the back of her left knee. Her jewellery is just a bit awry, her eyes somewhat bleary, the colour of her lips smeared, her gait unsteady with tiredness, yet she burns with promises, enflaming the passion of her young paramour, filling his head with suggestions and barely understood wants. He walks a little behind her, watching the seductive sway of her body. The door of her room opens and then closes with haste. I hear her throaty laugh bubble up before stopping suddenly.

In my own room I light the oil lamp and stare into the distance. The fort blazes with its thousands of torches and lamps making the rest of the city much darker by contrast. The emperor is away fighting one of the wars through which he is winning more and more territory each year. Agra is the seat of power and Emperor Akbar is the undisputed ruler, the king and refuge of the world.

The city is full of stories about its emperor, some true some, mythical. I have heard how he ascended to the throne at thirteen by decapitating his mortal enemy who was captured in battle and brought before him. His heart was unsure and his hand trembled for just an instant, then he severed the head from the body with one strong stroke and left his boyhood behind, forever. He was the son of Humayun, an ineffectual and weak king, but more importantly, he was the grandson of Babar, the fierce warrior Mughal, who had swept into Hindustan from his mountain home, changing its history and his forever. He traced his lineage from Timur and the Mongol hordes. However, unlike any of his forefathers, Emperor Akbar had integrated himself into the land he ruled, the people whom his ancestors had considered heathen.

I think about the emperor distractedly as I feel the square bundle of pink silk in my hands, trying not to listen to the dark silence from Nafasat Bai's bedroom. It is at night, away from the chores and the bustle of the day, that I return to my room and plumb my loneliness while wondering if even the king of the world, the Emperor Akbar, can return to me what I seek. If even he, with all his power, can rid me of my burden, for I can see the path ahead and I know that running away is not an option. My destiny travels with me like a demon on my back, sinking its claws into my flesh, refusing to let go.

Lovingly I turn back my sleeve, baring an unblemished patch of skin. I cut myself in a soft stabbing motion, almost like the too ardent kiss of an inconsiderate lover. The blood seeps out slowly, spreading over my skin, warming and comforting me. I wipe it away gently and feel sleep arrive like an incoming tide lured by the pull of the full moon. I fall asleep to the music of the gathering wind that blows through the night and glides over my body.

6

Lessons Unlearned

I have learned many lessons in my journey and I recite them to myself every day, so that they do not escape from me as easily as my life had. After freeing the Dom Raja from his body I had crept away, silent as a shadow. His body was still warm when I kissed his forehead, closed his eyes that were glazing over, his limbs moving spasmodically, and I had slipped away. His breath was still coming, jerky and random as I left him there, lying on the floor of the room that had been my refuge. His image remains with me: I can see the blood spilling out slowly from his body, wetting the ground in a red sheet, its warm stickiness drying and flaking on my hands, the blade still stuck at an angle in his body. I had learned to kill and I realized it took no special talent or even true intent, just desire, need and a handy weapon.

Even in the grey fog of my mind, I knew I had to leave before they – his servants found him – and me. I had murdered the most powerful man in Kashi and I would be, should be punished, harshly. They would not want to listen to my justifications and explanations nor to the truth that he had asked me, though he had spoken no words, to redeem him and set him free. They would not believe that I had done what was destined. I could not let his army of death attendants find me with his cooling body, his blood colouring my hands like bridal henna, and so I ran away, melting into the darkness, becoming one with the night.

I ran with nothing more than my square of silk, my bedraggled feather and discarded nosering, my memories and my scars. As I wandered through the countryside I knew that my appearance made people cringe and avert their eyes and I learned that I had power, just as the Dom Raja had said. The power of my fractured mind and muttered ramblings and my ability to put into often-cryptic words what I was thinking, to foretell the future, became my weapons and my tools. I had created within myself the power to become invisible within a crowd, moving among people while they remained unaware of my presence, like the shadow of a ghost. No one noticed me unless I wanted them to, until I made them.

Slowly I also learned how to hide what I did not want people to know about me. My mother would have been happy at the speed with which I learned to speak in half-truths and lies. My father, as always, would have smiled softly for he would know that these are talents born of necessity and need. I close my eyes and again imagine my life as it could have been if my destiny had been different. Perhaps by now I would have had a child, maybe two: a girl and a boy. I try to name them but I cannot. I try to draw their faces but I fail. They remain nameless and faceless but I can hear their baby prattle, their babble ringing loudly calling me, 'Amma, Amma.' They are not real and I cannot answer them so I stick my fingers into my ears to drown out their persistent sounds.

Then the Dom Raja invades my consciousness. His sightless, dead eyes bore into me and accuse me of betraying his trust and depriving him of his true redemption. He is confusing me, trying to trick me when both he and I know the truth.

I want all these images, these thoughts and feelings to leave me but they continue to flow in, battering against the fragile defences of my mind. Again I wonder where my husband's rotting body lies. Is there anything left? Any scrap of bone or flesh? And if I ever found anything of his body would I recognize it? A wife should recognize every part of her husband, even if he is dead and I know I would not. I feel that failure keenly within me.

I have learned, in my travels, that people want to know what the future holds, however vague is my telling of it. I have learned to spin stories, sprinkle them with my foreknowledge and my imagination and feed them to those hungering to know. It is the only way I know to eat and to survive.

I have told barren women they would have a son even if I neglected to tell them he would be stillborn. I have predicted marriages though I have not said they would be happy ones. People want to know only what they want and I have made my foreknowledge handy merchandise.

I have learned to stop predicting the weather. Even though I had foreseen the massive rains that had destroyed my life, I had not been able to conceive the magnitude of the tragedy that would befall me. Though I had known that something would change my life forever I had not realized it meant the destruction of everything familiar, everything that was mine. The Ganga and the wanton monsoon rains had killed my family and I could not bear to predict the fury of the weather for it was still too painful, like a wound not yet scabbed over.

Here, in Agra, far away from the Ganga, I try to break free from her clutches. Still sometimes, I think I can hear her taunting, knowing rhythmic whispers. I know I am hallucinating for Ganga is miles away and I live in a house far away, shielded from her suggestions through routine and work. I am safe, for a while.

As I had wandered the countryside, sleeping in the emperor's inns or in fields, I thought often about the Dom Raja. I missed his live, vital presence in my life: his nightly visits, our whispered conversations and the feel of his rough-pebbled skin on mine, the feeling inside me as I felt his presence surround and protect me. I wondered about his children and his wife, whose voices I had heard through the wall that had separated us. They had been a part of his life the way I had never been, their realness had robbed me of reason and the hope of a future.

In death I have made him part of my life. There is not a day that I do not think about him. Sometimes I close my eyes, bring up the end of my braid and brush it against my upper lip so it feels like the bristle of his moustache when he had kissed me.

I have marked myself for him, to tell the story of his presence in my life, commemorating his place on my body and in my life. I have made the mark under my left breast, mimicking the place where I had plunged the scythe into his body, the spot from where his soul had departed. It is the deepest cut I have made on myself. It stands for him, for Kashi and for our brief time together. It stands for the dream of the future I had wanted with him.

~

The house is coming alive in the late morning. I hear voices practicing songs, reciting aloud new poetry or giving orders to the servants. In a strange way, this house of women reminds me of Meera Ghat. Only here, time is not spent in yearning for death but in dreading the end of youth and beauty and the loss of money.

I help Nafasat Bai with her morning toilet. Her young lover has left early and her room looks empty and forlorn. She looks drained, different somehow, from the radiant courtesan of last evening. I can see tiny lines on her skin and the pores that were usually invisible seem rougher, larger and more apparent.

'He loves me he said,' she says more to herself than to me, as our eyes meet in the mirror.

I do not know how to respond.

'I grow tired of living life this way, Nadee. How long can I go on?'

I shrug in response as the comb winds its way through her tangled hair, stopping at each knot that has been created by his young, greedy hands grasping at moments and sensations.

'Do I love him?' she asks again

'Or do you just want to love him?' I ask.

'What do you mean?' her voice trembles a bit.

'Do you say you love him to justify your own needs? So that you can find a way to get out of this life – and he is perhaps the path?' I have learned to roll my meanings inside questions, hiding the intent of my foreknowledge. It is less direct this way, less painful, easier.

She laughs. 'Ah, you mad girl. You ask maddening questions. Here help me with this earring. It got twisted during the night.'

I untangle one of the strands of pearls that dangle from her earrings, trying not to hurt her as I tug it into shape. She continues talking. I learn that tonight her lover will not be coming.

'I wish I did not have to perform tonight, but I have to. My heart will not be in it, after all, since he will not be there. But Amma has said that I must because important people are coming.' Important people come every day and Nafasat is the main attraction, the main draw.

Tonight her voice shines with the intensity of her longing as she sings of keen separations that bite through her like the sweet pain of a knife's assault. She tells him, her absent lover, of the ache in her heart and body, the longing of her eyes to behold him. He has intoxicated her senses, he is a curse, his love an obsession that only death can cure.

Her audience is spellbound. She sparkles with a muted lustre and the sadness in her throbbing voice and her dark eyes makes her even more beautiful, more desirable, more worth possessing. She personifies the longing of love and desire and every man in the room wants her, even if it is just for a moment.

I can see that in the way their eyes, glazed with alcohol, follow her every move. I know it because Nafasat sings until the early hours of the morning and the other courtesans never get a chance to perform that night. Her audience does not allow her to leave and she is as much their slave as they are hers.

Velvet bags filled with gold coins are piled at her feet. Some of her admirers have torn away their diamond and ruby rings of solid gold and given them to her, tangled as they are in her sensuous web. She fields the propositions with skilled archness, pleading tiredness. Ever the consummate courtesan she bruises no egos and hurts no feelings.

Late morning brings with it letters and more gifts. They range from the lascivious to the poetic to the pragmatic. Her previous lover, a highly placed noble wants to give her a house. Even though she had jilted him in favour of the young nawab he still wants her. She would never have to perform again except for him. Jewels, servants and untold luxuries would be hers as his mistress. This is the moment of which courtesans dream, the fulfilled quest for escape and long-term stability. She knows that this is the way out, the only respectable way out for a courtesan. She can accept the generous offer or watch her beauty and talent wither and her patrons deflect their affections to another. Then she would be relegated to one of the small upstairs rooms where retired courtesans live out their lives in sad solitude.

The women upstairs are invisible to the rest of the house and to the world. Rarely seen, they are blurred reflections of themselves from earlier times. Their longing for their lost youth and past beauty can be seen only in the vibrant clothes and jewellery some of them wear, creating grotesque caricatures of their former selves. Time is a shifting desert landscape, desiccating youth and beauty in its unrelenting, unstoppable and unspeakably cruel progress.

In this house where talent and beauty are commerce, it is important to grasp opportunities with both hands and recognize the right time to leave. Still Nafasat cannot bring herself to respond to the letter she had tucked away in her room until she had fully formulated her plan. Her lover is coming tonight and she finds herself counting the minutes as never before. Her step is lighter and she seems younger and more beautiful. She takes extra care with her preparations today. Her eyes gleam seductively as her hips sway unspoken invitations to him. Tonight she sings of the maddening joy of meeting, of the feelings and emotions and thoughts racing through her veins, through every pore of her body as she prepares to rest her eyes upon him. The anticipation of satiation thrills through her voice today, not the sadness of separation.

She plans to have her young nawab read the proposition from the noble as an ultimatum. He would need to take her away from the house and set her up himself or she would accept the nobleman's offer. Her lover's offer need not be as generous and extravagant as the older noble's. A smaller house would do, fewer servants and lesser luxuries suffice. After all, she has jewellery to last a lifetime and does not desire any more; what is more important is spending her time and whatever portion of her life she desires, with him. She is excited at the prospect of leaving, of not watching her place being usurped when age finally claimed her looks, of not being victimized by the unstoppable tide of time.

'Do not do it,' I tell her, forgetting to phrase it as a question, as an icy fear invades my blood, chilling my body from the inside out.

'Oof, you are too cautious,' she smiles at me.

'What if… if he refuses?' I ask.

'He loves me. He said he did. And he wants to be with me. How can he refuse me then?' her voice is confident and unafraid.

'Still, what if he does?'

'Then I will accept the nobleman's offer and I will still be free of this place.' She laughs as if she knows it will never come to that. Her eyes fill with dreams about her nawab and their life together. He is rich. He says he loves her and she is sure he will not want to lose her. She is confident he will match the offer.

I know that things will not work out as she has planned. I also have learned that destiny will not be stopped or interfered with. I am powerless to stop her.

Her poems tonight sing of love and its satisfied aftermath. In her effortless, lyrical way she spins scenarios of passion and delicacy. She sings directly to her young nawab and tenderly kisses the velvet bag he bestows upon her, before placing it in the pile at her feet. She does not kiss any of the other gifts.

I see Amma frown at this wanton disregard for propriety. A courtesan does not, should not alienate her well-wishers by ignoring them in favour of a current lover.

Still her voice holds them all spellbound as usual and her lover smiles with satisfaction and pride, his heavy-lidded eyes promising her things he should not promise. Nafasat hangs all her hopes and dreams on them.

The evening meanders to an end. Stragglers stumble out finally, their steps held hostage to alcohol, walking unsteadily in a daze of unfulfilled sensual anticipation. Nafasat Bai's lover remains, staring at her silently. She lowers then raises her eyes to look into his, as the last person finally leaves and their hunger reaches across the room and touches.

In their usual ritualistic dance of seduction, she approaches him.

'I trust you were not too bored tonight, nawab sahib.'

'Nafasat Bai, only a fool or a blind and deaf man would dare say that to you.' His voice is deep and hints at his longing for her.

'The night is over. Perhaps you need to go home?' She speaks as if she already knows the answer to that.

'The night is just beginning, Nafasat Bai,' he laughs, confident of his attraction.

Playing the eternal roles of seductress and seduced, she turns and he follows her.

I hear her light laughter trill and mingle with his deeper tones. Her door opens and then closes hurriedly as if they can barely contain themselves. Earlier in the evening I had been in her room and had placed the things she had requested. A flagon of wine to prolong the intoxication of the evening, green paan topped with quivering silver leaf just the way he liked it, sprinkled with rose water. Fresh, whole fruit ready to be peeled and sectioned by the accompanying sharp, silver knife, its handle adorned with jade and turquoise. Chilled milk flavoured with almonds and pistachios for prolonged stamina and virility. I had daubed the sheets with her rose perfume and sprinkled red rose petals on their white, taut surface.

Later, as I pass by her door, I hear silence heavy with a message I dread to decipher. My heart thuds within me like a drum, beating a tattoo of panic and fear. I drift into an uneasy sleep, trying to remain aware of everything around me, waiting for a sound or a signal but my eyelids are weighted with tiredness and I am drawn into the depths of slumber.

~

The angry buzz of their conversation tunnels into the layers of my sleep and awakens me. I cannot make out the words from where I lie in bed, but the tones are unmistakable. For the first time since they have been lovers, the nawab and Nafasat Bai are arguing. More than arguing, they are fighting. His voice, deep and angry is louder than hers, as if he did not care who might be eavesdropping.

Her voice ranges from pleading to haughty to seductive and cajoling, but always soft, trying not to awaken the house. Tones of mock anger hide her desperation and true fears. His voice sounds by turns, wounded and hurt and then blisteringly furious, as if once unchained his rage would know no bounds.

The voices continue well into the morning, culminating in shouts and thuds. I can hear only his voice now as if hers was somehow silenced or muted. I know that the entire house is now awake and listening, though none dare intervene. Fights among lovers were common here, especially toward the end of an affair and the least we could do was to grant them some privacy.

The sounds end abruptly as if shut off midstream. Her door opens and closes with a bang and I hear his steps thudding down the hallway as he runs away from her. The sound of his loud, ragged breathing throbs in the narrow corridor long after he had opened the front door and dashed out.

When I approach the door of her room, with dread in my heart, I slip and fall on his bloody footprints, the imprint of his bare feet perfectly outlined in red. From Nafasat Bai's room, down the hallway and leading outdoors, his feet have tracked blood in shades ranging from crimson to the faintly pink prints near the front door. The house erupts in shouts, cries and curses and thudding feet running this way and that. I open the door and walk in, knowing what I would find yet utterly unprepared for the lessons still left to be learned.

7

Eleven Stairs

A giant red flower has bloomed in an obscene splatter on the low white ceiling of her room. Sluggish trickles of her life-blood roll down the walls in streaks and splashes, flowing together in streams into the river of blood in which she lies. I can hear the sound of her struggling breath, like moth wings weakly beating inside a glass jar, as she lies on her crimson-soaked bed, still alive. It seems impossible. How could so much blood flow out of her without killing her?

She breathes in gasps, trying desperately to cling on to life. The wound in her throat is gruesome, a second mouth that gapes like a wide, demented smile. I wad up a sheet using it to hold the lips of the gash closed, her head held tight in my lap. Her blood stains my clothes and my skin until it seems as if I bleed with her

~

I remember the events afterwards as if through a haze, as if they did not really happen. My universe was concentrated in that room, on that woman and her wounds. Still what was happening around me penetrated in bursts. Shouts and cries echoed all around, doors slammed, people fainted and wailed loudly as they waited for her to die. She refused. Even as blood seeped from every cut on her body, she held on, struggling to remain alive, trying to capture the air around her, squeezing it into her lungs to breathe. I caressed her hair, matted with blood, disarrayed where it had been grabbed, pulled and twisted painfully. For an instant she opened her eyes, wide with panic, pain and fear, and looked into mine. I smiled comfortingly at her, letting my foreknowledge glisten through. She relaxed then, allowing unconsciousness to drag her to its merciful lair. I rocked her in my lap, holding the sheet to her throat tightly, watching the cloth change from white to red, as each fiber was saturated with her blood.

By the time the physician arrived she was weak and unresponsive, though her breath came still, reedy and spluttering. He bandaged her wounds with ancient healing herbs, closing the one in her throat first with needle and twine. He worked in silence, shaking his head in disbelief. 'I cannot say anything. She should be dead already but she is not. A miracle indeed. The next day shall tell.' He left.

The ancient remedies worked, the blood stopped flowing out of her body and now everyone waited to see how long she would remain alive. For several tortured nights and days her body burned with fever as it fought off onslaughts of infections but still she hung on, refusing to die. I looked after her, wiping her burning brow with cold water and tending to her wounds, slathering on more of the healing paste. I crooned to her like a mother because responding to her pain and helping to ease it made me forget some of my own, sometimes. We were indeed alike now, Nafasat with her wounds of demented love and I with my self-inflicted marks that were my stories and memories. It had happened, we were as one person. She was no longer a beautiful temptress. And I had never been one. She was starting to keep her eyes open for longer periods of time now and opened and closed her mouth weakly trying to talk.

'Fifty… six,' she whispered. Her voice sounded scraped and raw, rusty and unfamiliar.

'What?' I asked her in a soft voice, unable to alter the volume of this exchange.

'He stabbed me fifty-six times. Fifty-six knife wounds in my body. I felt each one… each one. I counted. I counted because that is all I could do.' She drifted off on the last word, leaving it hanging in the air like cold droplets of condensed water, an accusation bathed in love and despair.

Her body had been her trade and now it was ruined. Nafasat Bai, the peerless courtesan of Agra was dead, even if her mangled body still lived. Every woman, including the empress who had held her husband back with black magic spells could now heave a sigh of relief and give thanks. The threat that was Nafasat Bai was humbled, annihilated and destroyed.

~

Today she is awake, though her eyes are fixed on the freshly scrubbed wall that nevertheless still bears the ghostly shadow-stains of her own blood. She has not yet seen herself in a mirror because Amma Jaan has asked for black cloths to be draped on the surface of every mirror in her room. Nafasat, for someone who once spent so much time gazing at her own reflection, critiquing and perfecting herself, now seems curiously untouched by their veiled appearance.

I know that she is not indifferent: she does not want to see, does not want to know because she is trying to escape the inevitability. The mirror that had always reflected her smouldering beauty would now show her a monster. The healed gash in her throat is not the deepest of her scars and even it appears as a dark coloured rope around her neck. Other scars are healing into dark, deep gouges where the flesh is missing, or shallower marks like silvery snakes forever embedded into her skin. Her voice at least appears to be untouched, stirring back to life as she recovers. As she grows stronger that much is apparent. He has left her vocal chords unscarred. As if even he, her jealous lover mad with rage, could not bear to extinguish her essence.

After a few more weeks it is time for her to move from her room. They are moving her to an upstairs room, next to the grey shadowy women whose presence she had always wanted to escape. Her old room was to be given to one of her many rivals. Amma looks at the ground while giving her the news.

'Nafasat Bai, you are like my daughter. In fact I feel you are my daughter. I want to make sure you are looked after, just as you have contributed to this house for years.' Her voice is sincere, though troubled.

The scarred woman on her bed looks at her with silent eyes.

'It will be much easier for you up there. Away from prying eyes and you can… you can take this girl with you. She will look after you. You will want for nothing. And, who knows?' She forces a laugh, 'when you are better, you may be back here. So you just concentrate on getting better and stronger.' The placating and uncomfortably indulgent tone of her voice dies away.

'Thank you,' Nafasat Bai's voice emerges from her ugly twin.

'Good, good. You are a sensible girl. Of course you understand.' Awkwardly Amma pats Nafasat's hair before leaving.

'Remember, you let me know if you need anything,' she says as she stops at the door.

'I will,' is Nafasat's response. As I pat her brow with a damp cloth I feel the fine tremor that vibrates through her entire body as she fights to keep her voice level and the tears at bay.

Four men are needed to carry her, lying on a light string cot, up the stairs to her new room. I hold her arm as we navigate our way upstairs for she clutches the sides of the cot like a frightened child. The climb is slow and painful as the men try not to jar the woman on the cot. The bones of her arm feel like dry twigs and I am afraid of snapping them into many pieces. I look at her face and see that her eyes are shut tightly, avoiding the avid gazes of the household as they watch her depart.

She is leaving behind forever, the section of the house where things happen, where laughter and music and hurriedly-snatched love exist, where life bubbles up through everything. She has to climb up eleven steps to her new life. Eleven steps separate youth, beauty and vitality from old worn-out shadows. Eleven steps lie between dreams and despair. With each step the tremors in her body grow more pronounced and I tighten my grip on her, willing her to grasp at my own strength.

She had always dreamt of leaving this house in a palanquin, like a bride leaving for her new husband's home, full of anticipation, a palpitating fear washed over by a vast sense of relief.

Experiencing the euphoria of escape. But this… these eleven steps had never been part of her plan. She asks the men to stop as we ascend the ninth step. She looks back once at the courtyard full of people and sees the doorway of her old room standing ajar, the chilman rolled up and out of the way. She can see into the room. It is empty.

They are starting to stamp out her existence. The only traces of her that still remain in her empty room are the dying echoes of her bloodstains which will be painted over today, obliterating her presence from that space. But today those faded marks tell stories about her life and her existence in loud whispers, battering against the walls of her tragic present. Nafasat Bai, peerless beauty, seduction personified, with the pained soul and voice of a fallen angel is dead, awash in a sea of pain and betrayed love. Only she and I can hear any of this. She lies back and the men know it is time to move on.

Her arm shakes in mine as we climb on to the eleventh step. It is a step that swerves into the curving wall and hides from view the courtyard below. We stand on an open terrace courtyard facing nine closed doors and one half-open one that surround the large space on three sides.

We head for the half-open door and step into a darkened room. It takes our eyes some time to adjust to it and we can see all her furniture and belongings have been piled together into the room until there is barely space to move. Her bed is ready and she is transferred to it after which the men leave. Again she closes her eyes tight and I wonder what she is thinking as she and I measure the deep silence of this new place.

She is crying. For the first time since the incident, she is crying. Silent sobs wrack the wreckage of her body and her tears run down her cheeks like twin rivers.

Unsure about what to do, I wait. Despite myself and despite her naked pain I want her to tell me what happened. I know it already but I feel it is important for her to tell me, in her own words though I do not know how to ask her. I cannot find the right words to ask her about the death of her dreams and the destruction of her desires because I am not sure those words exist. I touch the place close to my heart where I carry the tattered remnants of my own life and gather the strength and the patience to wait until she is ready to tell me.

'I wish he had killed me,' her voice quavers.

I remain silent still unsure how to respond. What is the right response to that wish? How many times had I wished that Ganga had killed me? I had woven elaborate fantasies of my own death: freedom from pain, from feeling, from foolish hopes, freedom from feeling dead inside. I sense what she feels but I cannot tell her for she has to feel what she does without borrowing from my own fractured hopes and torn emotions.

Days and nights pass slowly, painfully. Then one day the story flows from her like an unstoppable torrent, the words tumbling over each other in their eagerness to be said. I can tell she has relived that night a thousand times and now she is ready to invite me in to bear witness to those events that had taken her to this journey of eleven steps.

She tells me that he looked at her blankly when she had broached the subject. She had known that this was the performance of her life, her future hinged on it and she used all the wiles and skills she had amassed through the years. She giggled and flirted, enticing him to forget everything in the perfumed, soft seduction of her body, trying to weaken his will and prevail upon the victory of lust over practicality.

'Then I showed him that letter, from the nobleman… my old benefactor. Just to make him jealous, to make him understand that I was serious and sincere in my desire to leave this place forever, to have a new, a… another life. I said was willing to settle for less if he wanted me for himself, that I would send a refusal to the nobleman if only he would take me away himself. I told him of a dream in which we walked through a scented garden at night, just him and me. Fireflies flirted in the starless darkness and we made love under the shadow of a giant tree on the soft earth and smelled the fragrance of mogra. He stopped my descriptions with a slap that knocked me to the floor. He was beyond listening, beyond reason… beyond anger, like something within him had broken and could not be put back together.'

She draws a breath that reverberates loudly through her body before continuing, 'He screamed at me, "You want to leave? You want a house, money, a contract? I can take care of that." He said if he was not enough for me, that if I was truly just a whore who was looking for the highest bidder...' Her weeping continued but she went on as if compelled, 'that... that he would teach me a lesson. A lesson on how whores should never forget their station, always remember who they are. "No one will want you when I am done," he said. And then he smiled. He smiled at me as I begged him to stop, as I said... said that it was all right that we could continue as before. He laughed softly when he picked up the fruit knife and grasped my hair in his other hand so that I could not move my head. He laughed at the fear on my face. I whispered so I wouldn't disturb anyone. I thought he was joking, trying to scare me. That he would stop and everything would return to what it had been. I love... him. After a long time I had let myself fall in love. So I didn't scream. I didn't scream. And then I couldn't scream.'

I sit on the floor by the bed and see the frozen tableau in my head, exactly as she describes it. The knife gleams silver in his hand for an instant. Then it is awash in blood as his hand comes down fifty-six times, opening a new wound on her body each time, sometimes slashing, sometimes cutting, sometimes stabbing. The fifty-sixth is the long gash in her throat. He made sure it stopped short of being a mortal wound by slanting the knife just so and not using the sharp tip to gouge deeply and sever her main artery, her windpipe or her vocal chords. Or maybe by this time he just lacked the strength or the will to inflict further damage. As if even in the madness of his rage he could not bear to destroy all of her. He wanted her to live.

I know he has the knife still. He keeps it as a reminder of her. He has wiped away her blood with a silken handkerchief and keeps that and the knife hidden away, at his bosom. He loves her so desperately, so greedily that the thought of Nafasat being touched by any man made him go mad. That she would even allow herself to think of such a thing after having been with him. The thought that someone else might claim her as his own, make love to her, listen to her sing in privacy away from the crowds was too much for him to bear. He wanted to make her his, only his, and forever, and by his act, he changed their fates, binding them together with a thread of a thousand strengths.

Every time she now looks at her body she cannot help but think of him, feel him, even if she tries not to. Each time she moves and feels pain, her heart is drawn to his permanent presence in her life and she feels close to him. Nafasat draws strength from these thoughts for she smiles as she tells me, 'He proved he loves me, that he truly loves me.'

Every day she examines her body in the uncovered mirror, as if hoping that by some miracle she will find her beauty pristine and her skin unmarked. One day I show her my scars, just some of them, in sharing and commiseration and to fulfil some other needs I cannot comprehend. But they are less impressive than hers, not as deep and not as spectacular. And I have always been careful not to mark my face and neck and other parts that can be seen by others. Ganga's scar on my forehead is the only one visible to all who look at me. The baring of my own pain offers her no solace. She cannot look past the shallowness of my physical marks into the dark place within me where scars run so deep that they cannot be seen, the place which makes me mark myself everyday. She ignores my attempts at empathy and remains wrapped inside her agony.

Her scars are deep, dark depressions in her skin and as they heal they grow uglier and more permanent. She has nightmares at night where they converge into one giant scar and begin to consume her and she tries to fight, lashing out with her hands. I shake her shoulder vigorously to make her stop and she comes awake gurgling as if she is choking on blood, crying in terror and fighting, locked in the battle to save herself.

I sleep in her room, in the corner, on a rough mat as I tend her on her journey to recovery. She has entered a detached state where she is biddable and amazingly calm as if she is not really there. Her lips move and I can barely make out what she says as if reciting a prayer, 'He loves me. He will come and get me. He loves me. He will come and get me.'

'Stop! Stop!' My hands try to pinch her lips shut, blocking out those demented words but the words slip past my fingers and spill into the room, filling it with their odd, mad cadence. She smiles widely as if she has won a battle.

I feed her and bathe her and do all the things that mothers do, letting the knowledge of our secret pains wash into each other until sometimes I cannot distinguish between them. The path she is destined to follow is long and confusing and she needs to be prepared. Her voice will be her salvation. It is the only part of her past life that has survived. This I know.

~

The wide, red-mouthed gash etched into a creamy, unblemished throat smiles at me with glee. It sounds out its words like wine splashing into a goblet, 'he loves me still, I know it. He will take me away from all this.' I am trapped in this dream without a voice, without the ability to scream. I try to break the spell that holds me mute and helpless, to no avail. The lips of the wound move with sensuous seduction,

Death comes to us all, my love,
Soon I shall meet you in paradise
And ask you why
You went away and left me
Here alone.
I await you, awash in blood.

My voice gushes back into my throat with a flood-like force and then I cannot stop screaming. The screams burst out of my throat, tearing at the fragile, wet tissues, bubbling out of the depths of my being.

'Nadee, Nadee,' Nafasat's voice bleeds into my unconsciousness and awakens me. Frantically I touch my own throat relieved to find it whole. In the darkness I cannot see Nafasat though I know she is straining to look at me.

'I… I am… all right. I am fine. Go to… go to sleep.' I whisper in a shudder that tears through me. The room is silent now as both of us try hard to be quiet.

I fall asleep again slowly, drifting into the waves that lap at my conscious mind. I slow my breathing and see Nafasat's life unfold inside my mind like a flower. As I try to relax, entombed inside the darkness, I hear her breathing deepen as gradually she falls into a long-postponed rest.

The wet strands of the water hyacinth entwine themselves around me and take me on a journey to meet my own denied life. This time the Dom Raja's whispers mingle with the shouts of the others who beg me to free them. I feel his rough kisses on my scars making me vibrate with an ecstasy that for a moment overshadows the pain of loss. I come awake once more and I fear I shall never sleep again, for a strange panic rustles to restless life within me. My tiredness prohibits me from deciphering its meaning and I can only wait helplessly, caught in a mesh of darkness, waiting for dawn to deliver me into the arms of a new day. I awaken, as always, awash in a river of tears.

8

Chhappan Chhoori: Fifty-Six Knives

It is astonishing the damage that a small fruit knife can do to a body when used with passion and focused anger, what its shiny blade can do to muscles and sinew and flesh. Her lover's knife has cut into flesh that will never regenerate, severed connections that can never be repaired, made irrevocable changes in her body and face. Nafasat's body shakes with fine tremors that are not the result, as I had originally thought, only of pain though her physical pain and her tremulous emotional state intensify the constant shaking. She can grasp nothing in her right hand and has no feeling in her left. Her face is as grotesque now as it had once been beautiful and I doubt most people could bear to look at it… at her…

Each day that she grows stronger she comes closer to the reality of her situation, the permanence of her state. Gradually she is being drawn into the sad, segregated fellowship of the two other residents of the rooms on the top floor. Their doors are opened only when their food is delivered from the kitchen. Sometimes I can hear the creaking of a rusty hinge and have glimpsed shadowy faces that stare at our half-open door. Only sometimes, at dusk they would emerge, walking slowly on the terrace, their steps heavy, infused with their solitude and their memories. These worn brown wooden surfaces, and the solitary existences of the women who live behind them, are calling out to Nafasat; they want to be the final reckoning of her life.

Nafasat is still in a state of fugue. When I force a morsel past her clenched lips she swallows, when I lift her arm to change her kurta she does not resist. She is in a place where she cannot be reached, where she reigns, still beautiful, unblemished and unmarked.

'He will come for me soon, won't he, Nadee?' she asks me every day, in a voice that is strangely normal, never waiting for a response before she continues, 'He loves me, of course. You don't know how much he loves me.' Then she laughs as her fingers trace the path of the scar on her throat, touching its rough bumpiness restlessly as if she feels her lover's caress.

I wonder what she will say if I look her straight in the eye and tell her that he will never come back, that he almost killed her. That he tried to kill her. Even the thought sounds cruel; if I gave voice to it, she would look at me with hurt, her large eyes staring at me through her maze of scars. A long, thin scar like the winding lash of a whip bisects her left eyelid and makes her face look lopsided. Nafasat Bai's clear brown-black eyes look out at me from the ugly, masked face of a stranger.

She has put away the bright, beautiful clothes, the plumage of her butterfly-like existence and exchanged them for dull greys, browns and blacks, as if she wants to melt into the shadows that till now had lurked only at the outskirts of her life.

Every day, to fill the growing boredom, we work on her recovery. She has started to walk now, her legs with their depleted strength trembling at the slightest jolt, her entire body wincing in pain. Her eyes fill with tears as she remembers her effortless dancing, when her feet could stamp the hard marble floors for hours, pounding out rhythms of passion and love. She wants to give up often but the same force that did not let her die makes her continue to try. Each time she collapses into defeat she makes herself get up and go on. Perhaps she feels the touch of her lover's hand on her shoulder, urging her sweetly to continue and like always she cannot resist him.

As I continue helping her I know that things are about to change again and I am not sure how she will handle it. What will she do when she hears of the news whose restless fluttering inside me makes me want to hold her to my heart and shield her from more agony? Soon she will find out what I have known for days now.

Her lover's body was discovered face down in a ditch, five days ago. After wandering the countryside for months he was finally dead. His young wife, pregnant with their first child, was now the widow of a husband she barely knew and surely never loved. His body was emaciated, his beard untrimmed until it grew wildly about his face, hiding the features Nafasat Bai had loved to look upon and touch. There really had been no need for him to run away for he would have faced no consequences for attacking a courtesan, even if she was the most famous in all of Agra. Still he had been compelled to escape what he had done. The part of him that could not believe his passion and love had been distilled into maddened rage had terrified himself most of all.

So he ran, with the blood-stained fruit knife that had cleaved into her skin still in his hand. The splatters of her blood dried onto his skin, seeping into his pores, becoming one with him as never before. As if she was indeed his for all time. No one knew if the nawab sahib had killed himself or if he had been murdered for his jewellery and money. His throat had been cut, severed from ear to ear, colouring the water in the ditch red. The fruit knife had sunk into the shallows beside him as his life poured out around him.

Nafasat Bai's cry when she was finally given the news was like the keening sound of the wind during a storm. She came out of her dream-trance like state in an instant, as she tore at her hair and beat her head against the ground in her anguish. Tears ran down her cheek in torrents, mixing with the blood from the wound she had opened on her forehead, and she cried until she hiccupped and gasped for breath. Still she could not stop.

She wept for hours, exhausting herself as she relived the loss of her love, of herself and of any hope she might have desperately clutched. The other doors on the courtyard came open as the two shadow-women inside listened to Nafasat Bai's outpouring of grief. Perhaps they took some solace in her loss and were pleased by it since they had nothing left to lose themselves. Perhaps the extinguishing of her last flickering of hope filled them with some perverse delight. Or perhaps they cried with her as they re-lived their own losses.

The dream, however unreal and remote, that her lover might return, proclaim his love and carry her away forever was shattered into a thousand pieces along with her broken heart and scarred body. So she returned to the only thing she had left, the only thing that had not abandoned her. For the first time in almost a year, Nafasat Bai awakened one morning and decided to sing.

~

Her voice is her link to her past, the bridge back to her sanity, to him and to the life she had lived. It reverberates with pathos as she sings songs about the death of love, of burning unspoken passion and the longing that is never satisfied and grows stronger, like a wave building deep under the ocean and crashing into shore, destroying everything in its wake. Each morning she sings for hours, lost in her art, giving voice to her grief and love and loss. Her voice is more mature, more real somehow, cutting deep into the consciousness of any listener, giving voice to all the agony of loss in the world.

She no longer calls herself Nafasat Bai. Nafasat means delicacy, finesse, class and beauty and she no longer qualifies. She has grown beyond the confines of this persona, become more than its ingredients, surpassed what is needed for great courtesans. She has renamed herself, cutting the last link with her past life, commemorating her demented, rageful lover's place in her life forever. She calls herself Chhappan Chhoori, and when she sings the listener can hear the pain from each of those fifty-six knife wounds on her body, as if they were freshly made and filled with her life-blood.

She sings without stopping, as if in the absence of everything else, her music is what will resurrect her. She is right. I listen to her, spellbound and watch as she transcends her scars and her tremors and her deformed face to become more than Nafasat ever was, more than Nafasat could have ever hoped to be. She no longer leans on her beauty and her sparkling eyes, languidly letting them speak for her. Her voice is saturated with anguish and it stands on its own with no help. It has elevated Chhappan Chhoori to something more than a courtesan, more than a woman.

Her singing has become an obsession as once her love had been. In the evenings, when we hear the faint sounds of the mujra starting up, the strains of the sarangi and the beat of the tabla accompanying the manufactured sultry voice of the courtesan who is singing downstairs, she tries to restrain herself. She hums, she sings softly, biting her lips and tamping down her voice so as not to disturb the evening's performance. Until one night, when she can no longer hold back the magnificent torrent of her voice, she sits on the floor, closes her eyes, opens her mouth and sings.

She is singing out to her lover for she feels his absence as keenly as the winter wind that burrows into her clothes and cuts her flesh and her heart into ribbons. 'When will you come?' she asks in her song, 'When all that is left are these eyes which have been awaiting your arrival for so long? Will you come then?' Her voice undulates like a stream, then a torrent and carries with it the pent-up passion of every lover who has waited for another without giving up.

I am so captivated by her singing that I pay no attention to the abrupt cessation of the music from downstairs. I do not hear the sound of the footsteps that come up the stairs and stop in front of her half-open door. It is only when she stops and we both glance towards the door that we notice her audience, standing in the dark outside, while we sit inside by the flame of a single oil lamp.

The singer sits where she is, motionless, looking at them in silence. Finally, someone pushes the door fully open. In the crowd I can see Amma's face in which worry and irritation war with hope. As appreciation is showered upon the singer, hope wins out, as Amma realizes what I already know, that she has in her house that rarest of courtesans, one who does not have to rely on youth and beauty and wiles to draw men into her presence. Chhappan Chhoori has become a timeless courtesan.

Amma's portentous words, which, at the time, were meant merely to placate Nafasat Bai, before she ascended the eleven steps, were coming true. For the resurrected courtesan, Chhappan

Chhoori, was returning to her own world. She knew that her heart and her tortured body belonged to her dead love but there was something within her struggling to grasp at a last chance at life and if not happiness, then recognition, and her benefactors' appreciation was a balm to her raw and ragged soul. Word of Chhappan Chhoori's singing and the newly-minted beauty in her voice races through Agra, whetting the appetite for gossip. Gossip and rumours had flared in the months after the attack only to die down under the onslaught of news of the emperor's victory in the till-then unconquered territories of the south. People come, looking for the grotesque, drawn by the desire to watch a freak and they leave spellbound as they have never been before, slaves to her voice. They say over and over again: 'Chhappan Chhoori's voice transcends beauty, it goes beyond imagination and surpasses the mundane details of life and love.'

Business in the house has never been better, making Amma's lingering doubts dissolve. Chhappan Bai as she is formally called is back in her large room, her furniture exactly as it had always been. We descend those eleven steps in a manner much different than the journey of our ascent had been. Chhappan Bai walks down on her own strength, though she still grips my arm tightly for support. The other doors on the roof remain tightly shut and we do not even give them a backward glance. The sad and empty echoes of the past remain upstairs where they belong as we climb back down into the world of the living.

While this reborn courtesan pays special attention to her toilet again, she has never returned to the bright colours of her past. She refuses to dye her hair and the broad white streaks have become as much of her trademark as her scars. She does not camouflage the damage to her body, which shakes constantly, her scars displayed matter- of-factly, and she no longer dances. She sits in one place, her wide skirts spread around her, facing her audience, and sings, with her eyes closed tightly as if she is looking at someone or someplace far away. She opens her eyes only when the applause breaks around her like thunderclaps and quietly she expresses her thanks for her patrons' appreciation. Her eyes no longer flirt coyly but look straight into men's hearts, with a bold directness that leaves them with no defences and she draws them ever deeper into her clutches.

When she sings she retreats somewhere else into a place of deep silence and channels a voice that is not wholly hers. For even though I recognize the voice as that of the Nafasat Bai I know, I realize it is much beyond even her old capabilities, it is much more than she could have hoped for.

This is the voice they come to hear. The voice of pain that intertwines with love and beauty and shimmers with emotions shaded with delicate meanings that cannot be named or described. This is not the voice of Nafasat Bai or of Chhappan Chhoori; of any courtesan or woman. This is a voice.

Those among her court do not come to see a performance aided by dance and beauty. They come to pay homage to her talent, to the poems she writes and to her wondrous voice. Chhappan Chhoori has gone further than Nafasat Bai ever did or could have ever hoped to. She has become a living legend. Men journey from afar when they are confronted with the question, 'have you listened to Chhappan Bai of Agra?' and are forced to answer in the negative. Seeing her, listening to her, getting lost in the magic of her voice has become the mark of a true connoisseur, a true lover of art, music and beauty that transcends the physical. It seems her admirers have increased tenfold for there are nights when the hall overflows and we have to turn people away. As she counts the days of her newly resurrected life, a smile often plays on her scarred, misshapen lips. She no longer dreams of respectability and comfort and rest and a place where she can think about her lover for an eternity. Instead she is now cushioned by the admiration and love of genuine admirers of talent.

Something else remains, like an itch under my skin. My foreknowledge nudges me gently warning me of other things about to happen, of the stops on my own journey that lead to the inevitable end of my story.

~

It looks like an ordinary letter, written on thick, white paper, rolled around a plain wooden rod and tied with a simple gold thread.

Nothing proclaims its importance except its bearer in whose brocade robes and flashing jewels we can see a pale reflection of the grandeur and majesty of the sender.

Chhappan's voice had slipped between the cracks of the fort's walls, flowed through the scented night and enraptured the emperor who had just returned from his southern campaign. News of his victories had spread through the city like water running downhill, swift and direct, and soon poems in his honour flooded the streets and markets. We had all heard them, bloated with hyperbole and high praise, never delving into the complex simplicities of what makes a king also a mortal man.

I imagine the scenarios in which the King of the World listens to Agra's voice, the beautiful pained songs of Chhappan Chhoori. I think of him inspecting his fort as he stands above the Yamuna, watching the river bathed in moonlight. His shoulders slump and he is tired, perhaps injuries received in battle plague him still. He has tired of the effusive welcome from his queens and nobles and is searching for some time to dream and to think, some space to visualize his greatest visions and plans. Then… hush… he wills his heart to beat softly, for he hears something borne on the currents of the wind.

A voice, aah such a voice, it flows like water and makes something buried deep inside him hurt and come to life. This voice uncovers his pain and starts to heal it and he knows that he has to listen to it more fully, to discover its source. And so here, in front of us, stands one of his messengers, requesting the pleasure of Chhappan Bai's company in the emperor's court. The emperor has sent an invitation which asks for the privilege of being her audience within the great halls of the red fort of Agra to celebrate the kingdom's victory over the stubborn southern states.

It is an invitation that no one else in the house could even have dreamed of or dared to imagine. No such messenger had ever entered this house, with such a missive for a courtesan, an invitation from an emperor.

The emperor, the Refuge and King of the World, Jalal-ud-din Akbar has requested the pleasure of Chhappan Bai's presence at his court. He has commanded her to sing for him and his court, so that he too can listen to the famous voice of Agra, in person and not just grasp at the furtive melodies that drift his way in the dark.

~

For several nights now I struggle to fall asleep. My eyes are heavy, filled with the grit of too many sleepless nights and though I long for rest, I cannot settle into it. My sense of loss has not abandoned my soul and I wonder where I shall find all that has been taken from me..

As I wind a long strand of my hair around my finger, trying to lull myself to sleep, I am filled with the dread of certain change and I wonder what the emperor might say if I go to him as a humble petitioner. Is he able to return my life to me? I caress the handle of my knife-pen which has written many stories and secrets upon me. Tonight I lack the strength to add to my book of life. I sleep, exhausted.

9

Andaliib-e-Jahan: Nightingale of the World

Agra Fort, Winter, 1572

The Yamuna is a quivering, thin-bladed silver sword, snaking away in the night, flowing far below the walls of the fort. It flashes in the light of the moon as we arrive for Chhappan Chhoori's performance, the zenith of her career, the envy of every courtesan – every singer – in front of the Emperor of Hindustan.

In this night, lit with low hanging stars, blazing torches and flickering lamps the red sandstone glows radiantly pink-gold. The marble of the fountains and interior palaces reflects this rosy colour and the whole fort is awash in a blush, as if it too awaits the songs of a peerless entertainer. As if it too had heard her voice so many nights that the emotions trapped in that sound had pierced its stone exterior, finding the beating heart within.

Another voice throbs in the background, speaking in tones too low and secretive for anyone but me to hear and to understand. It is a voice distinctly familiar yet oddly alien and it rushes into me from many sides. Pools gush water into fountains that arc into tall sprays and diffused streams, sending splashing and gurgling sounds reverberating everywhere, entering my consciousness. As water falls from marble channels into large collecting ponds, the flowers and little lamps placed into the niches behind the falling sheets of the sparkling, clear liquid dissipate shimmers of diffused light and a faint perfume through the night air. I am oblivious to the beauty and majesty for I realize now whose voice speaks to me. The water is drawn up through an intricate system of aqueducts, channels and wells from the Yamuna and it is her presence I feel wrap around me.

She cuts through the tension and excitement, through the other voices and sounds that fill the great hall. I know that like Ganga, she too will become a part of my life, changing it in ways unforeseen. I feel the weight of her looming presence settle in my stomach like a great boulder. I know that she is a gentler force than that other river that altered the course of my life. Nevertheless, I work on relegating her whispers to remote long-unused corners of my mind, as I, along with everyone else get ready for Chhappan Bai's performance. Even Yamuna seems to hold her breath, her whispers falling low, as we await the commencement of this historic night.

There is an excitement in the air that can be touched, felt and savoured: this will be a night when secrets will be bared, plans unmasked and passions uncovered. I know that this is the night that destiny will begin to speak directly to me again as it divorces me from the links that have bound me to Agra and the house I live in.

Silks, velvets and brocades hiss and rustle in the great halls and gardens as we await the emperor's presence. The ladies of the fort, the harem, the girl children, old relatives and family retainers are already seated behind the heavy, barely fluttering curtains. They all sit in their designated sections, divided by status and birth and importance. I imagine the empress sitting among them, watching over the lower queens, giving orders to her slaves and servants, ignoring the multitudes of other women who do not matter in the least, rendering them invisible. Empress Jodha Bai, Mother of the World, daughter of the desert, princess of Rajputana and mother of the future emperor of Hindustan has withstood the assaults of many women upon her husband's heart. She shares him with a harem of three thousand – wives and concubines acquired through political alliances and physical lust. Now she waits to see Chhappan Chhoori, the one threat she had guarded against, the one invader who had drifted in like the wind, enflaming her husband's imagination and spirit. I wonder if she feels a sense of relief about Chhappan's lost beauty, those fabled flirtations and practiced charm. I wonder if she is curious; or merely relieved that now she has only a voice to contend with. She does not know that this Chhappan is far more dangerous to the imaginations of men, for she slips past their usual defences and desires, bringing them to their knees as her famed beauty never had, binding them to her for life.

~

'Tis not the chain of insanity on the neck of the afflicted Majnoon;
Love hath laid a loving hand on his neck.

Chhappan Bai's voice cuts through the night, severing all muttered conversations, chopping through sniggers about her ruined looks and rendering everyone speechless. She begins to sing as soon as the emperor, ensconced in silks and velvets, sits upon his throne and gestures to her to begin. The giant ruby in the emperor's turban sheds its scarlet fire into the night. He affectionately caresses the head of the little boy seated beside him, his love for the future crown prince shining through his gestures and his expression.

Emperor Akbar never gets a chance to fully look upon Chhappan Bai's lopsided eyes, her mismatched lips and the deep, dark gouges that have turned her face into a desolate moonscape. For as her voice flows out of her, he is aware of nothing but that sound and those words, moving in an effortless lyricism that fills the night with its melody of tragic love. She sings his own words, from a poem he had written once and abandoned. I am sure he wonders how she came by this poem, how she managed to find his writing, but it is a thought that stirs only to succumb to the spell of her voice. He along with others in the audience have become Majnoon, the mad lover, wandering, lost in the hot desert sand, the other half of the heart that is Laila; Majnoon whose thirst can only be quenched by being in the presence of his one true love.

As part of her entourage, I sit with the rest of her troupe, in the open, not hidden away behind the curtains as are the noble ladies of the court. Chhappan Bai sits directly in front of the emperor on a lavish Persian carpet, her head slightly bent; her eyes closed as always, her voice unusually spectacular. Her back is towards me and I can see the palsy that grips and shakes her without remorse, but leaves her voice untouched.

I am standing at a new curve in the journey of my life and I can just barely see past the bend or perhaps I am afraid to fully examine the ceaseless flow, too apprehensive about the approaching maelstrom. The emperor, Chhappan Bai and I are three points of a triangle and at this moment in time, we are aligned and I know that we are linked forever.

She sings all night and the court stays awake with her. I can tell the emperor weeps inside, caught up in the magic of her voice and the knowledge of the words she sings. She sings of the moment when she felt the world came to a stop, when creation died, the instant when her eyes met those of her love. This moment of the apocalypse when she felt her pulse quicken, her heart beat faster within her, was the moment of her doom. For all her battlements had been stormed, her being conquered, her soul enslaved and her quivering, fragile self was tender, defenceless and entirely at the mercy of her love. Love is the greatest betrayal of all, she sings.

Then she stops, as though drained of all song, all emotion. She is exhausted. Silence drops like a giant blanket. She finishes abruptly for she has sung all that she can sing tonight. She bows, her torso inclined into the rug on which she has sat for hours, unmoving.

The emperor descends from his throne and walks towards her. He is a tallish, stocky man, his skin darkened by the sun, his Mongol ancestors looking out at the world from his slightly slanted eyes. His face quivers with the strain to keep his emotions in check as he looks upon Chhappan Bai's bowed head.

'You have pleased us immensely,' he says. His court holds its breath at his speaking directly to a courtesan.

'From now, we will call you Andaliib-e-Jahan.' With reverence he detaches the giant ruby from his turban and hands it to her. She lifts her head slightly to take in his presence. The gem flashes red like blood, in her cupped hands and she kisses it before placing it by her side.

The emperor has renamed Chhappan Chhoori, the nightingale of the world and in his doing so she has claimed a territory outside the experience of any courtesan. This is the same court that boasts the presence of the immortal and legendary musician, Mian Tansen. The same emperor who values Tansen as the embodiment of music has recognized in the voice of a courtesan the power to stir hearts and souls.

I know, though I cannot see her face that tears are rolling down, flowing into her scars like salve until she can taste their salt. That salinity will forever be imprinted in her consciousness as the flavour of her ultimate triumph.

~

'See, she has lost all fear, she has conquered. Fear of loss… and fear of death,' the whisper snakes around me fluidly and I know the Yamuna has pushed her way into my life despite my best efforts and that she now flows deep inside me. I have tried to avoid her, tried to stay away from her shores.

It is of no use. For, it takes but one glimpse, one spray of her waters flung into the air with impudent ease, dampening my hair as I walk into the fort, one whisper in a black and silver night and I am undone.

Where the Ganga was passionate, haughty and angry, Yamuna is gentle and calm… seductive. Her whispers soothe me and I know that this journey with her will be different from any I have undertaken before. I close my eyes and surrender to her will with a sense almost of relief. I have missed another presence within me, felt as if there was something lost rattling around me that has again found an anchor.

I have lived through Nafasat and then through Chhappan, losing myself in the process, forsaking my quest for my own way and my life. Something within me tells me that Yamuna will point me towards the next intersection of my life. All she asks of me in return is that I listen to her, listen to her voice so that she can tell me her secrets. Secrets that I can add to the half-written, abandoned stories on my skin.

This night is the beginning of Chhappan's initial transformation. I have been so consumed with her care that I have neglected my own nightly rituals. Now her change is complete, her journey set on its unshakeable and unchangeable path, and I realize that my presence in her life is superfluous, a relic from an embarrassing time of pain, indignity and loss. A rush of anticipation warms my skin and I can feel the ghost-weight of steel in my hand, its coldness as it presses against me, and the warming comfort that always follows.

Since I had been drawn into the intricate web of this courtesan whom I had served in her two distinctly different forms I had lost something within myself that even Ganga had not taken from me. I had seen Chappan's image and mine coalesce briefly, becoming one, both of us with our marked bodies, our tortured, restless souls and our silent search for something beyond ourselves. For a while she had been the reflection I saw in the mirror and until tonight I had been comforted by the feeling of oneness, of understanding and of being understood.

But in this place, tonight, that mirror is shattered, for Chhappan Chhoori has claimed a place that can never be mine. She has something that I will never have and as her voice soars into the night I am never more aware of that truth. All bonds between us lie broken and a part of me cries within myself. It is not until I feel wetness on my loosely clasped palms do I know that, like Chhappan, I too am crying, but for reasons unlike hers, reasons that I cannot yet put into words.

The emperor will issue a proclamation early this morning, into a kingdom where the sun has not yet risen, in that indescribable time between night and dawn when the heavens stand still and wait for the earth to awaken. As courtiers proclaim the great victories that he has won in the south, as they describe the newly conquered length and breadth of the empire, we can only listen and feel the gradual heat of the sun as it climbs out of the depths of darkness and begins its ascent into the sky.

'Jahanpanah Badshah Akbar proclaims today, in front of his empire, that the move of the court to the new capital of Hindustan, the village of Sikri is almost complete. From this day forth Sikri shall be known as Fatehpur-Sikri, in commemoration of our latest victory. Tonight we are witness to the birth of a new city, the likes of which the world has not seen and it will be for all eternity a symbol of his reign and magnificence. Fatehpur-Sikri, the city of victory, the city of dreams is born tonight.'

All assembled are quiet. I have heard of this village, a distance away from Agra. We are all aware of its significance to the emperor. The streets of Agra are rife with stories of the miraculous birth of Prince Salim, who sits now, fast asleep, by his father's throne.

~

For years the emperor and his consorts had tried to produce an heir to the throne of Hindustan, a healthy male child. Without an heir this tenuous kingdom, won with blood and terror, alliances and wiles would be torn asunder: the least any great emperor desires is a legacy and that had been denied to him. When all natural methods and old-wives remedies failed they prayed in vain and were reduced to wishing for miracles. It was in the end a miracle that had given them the prince, a miracle in the personage of a simple man, the Sufi pir Salim Chishti of the little village of Sikri, surrounded by craggy hills and rough scrub.

Sheikh Salim Chishti was their last resort, the only unexplored hope and so the emperor and empress of Hindustan walked barefoot and humbled, into his little cave from where it was said he communed directly with God. They begged him for a son, to intercede on their behalf with Allah. He did. So the heir to the throne was born, a symbol of the helplessness of a monarch and named for the beggar saint whose prayers brought him into existence, Salim, the future emperor of Hindustan.

But he is still a boy, unaware of the demands and the weight of history, unknowing of the legacy that is his, unimpressed by the exploits of his forefathers. So he sits, nodding off to sleep, while the world inside and outside the fort readies itself for one of the biggest changes in history, and one of its greatest blunders.

As my fears blossom they flow together with an uneasy excitement into a viscous mixture that threatens to burn my insides with bile. I hear again Yamuna's voice in the silent void. I walk by her banks in the bluish evening light, unmissed in the excitement of the previous night's events. I dig into the cool, damp sand burying my feet under the tunnels I have made and listen to her secrets. And I tell her mine. No one has asked me for my secrets for a long time. Even as I listened to Chhappan Bai's confidences, ran her errands and attended to her needs, no one, not even she, had asked how I, Nadee, felt, what I looked for and what I wanted.

But tonight Yamuna coaxes my dreams and desires and hopes and fears out of me. I had kept them tightly locked away inside myself, for there had been no need to speak them out aloud. Until now. We communicate in silences and I fall asleep, relaxed, burrowing into the sand by her banks, as Yamuna sings a lullaby softly to me. A breeze picks up moisture and coolness from her waters and enters my dreams as a soothing balm, erasing my night terrors, whisking me away from the wet tendrils of the giant water hyacinth, saving me at least for one night.

10

Yamuna: River of Secrets

Slow your breathing and feel the sound of your blood rushing within you, hear it pound against your eardrums; close your eyes and imagine the slightest kiss of a patient lover; imagine yourself in a refuge within which there is no torment. There, shhhh… sshhhh… be patient, now… you can hear me, listen to me as I sound out my words like water, feel yourself being swirled around gently, enveloped in soft coolness. Yes, you are ready. You are ready to listen to me now.

Do you know what secrets are? Do not think about the question for too long; just say the answer out loud. I know, for I am made of them. Secrets are precious little nuggets you keep from others, that you hoard jealously within yourself, for they are storehouses of power. Sometimes they come disguised as weaknesses. That is how most people interpret them, as weaknesses that have the ability to destroy them.

There are a few, however, who have felt their power, even if they do not fully comprehend their value. This girl, Nadee, is one such, who feels as if she is drowning under the weight of her secrets, dragged down into some deep abyss from which there is no escape. Though she has glimpsed her power in flashes, she has not understood the invincibility of her secrets.

Then, there is me, Yamuna, the river-goddess. I gather secrets deep into my being and nurture them like precious children, for, like offspring, they are the progenitors of power. They hold the key to our collective futures. Secrets are like desires, deep, dark and dangerous, and they slither into every part of your life, your heart, mind and soul. Today, perhaps on this historic evening, it is time to tell you some of mine.

Forever I have seen the people of the earth enthralled with the beautiful, golden Ganga, a gift from heaven, supreme mother, nestling the souls of the dead, gathering their bodies into her bosom. They call me Ma too, but only as an afterthought. They do not know that I have secrets, secrets of power, that can rival any of Ganga's stories. They dwell within me in depths of quiet, waiting to be uncovered by those who are persistent and perceptive.

I, Yamuna, am the daughter of Surya, the Sun God. He rides his chariot that is pulled by seven horses across the sky and I am secure in the knowledge that he will slip exhausted, at the end of the day, into my embrace. I rejuvenate him each night as only a daughter can, with love, patience, and obedience so that he can start his relentless march all over again. I hold in my power the days of the Earth, its life-giving sun, its heat and the birth of all the things that grow in the ground and everything that is beautiful.

Ganga is the repository of the dead. Humans believe that she will take them with her to heaven, flowing over their sins, drowning their eternal punishments. They wade into her waters and pray for death, they pray they will die in her presence and so be assured of nirvana. They are afraid. Petrified of death and its terrible finality. Death is a dark shadow that terrorizes them, overflows into their days, oozing out from their nightmares, like an invading army of demons in the night, shaking human minds and bodies with bony hands. When death looks them straight in the face they know that it is too late and that all is lost.

In Prayag, where Ganga and I flow side by side before becoming one, I observe the fear in the faces of humans, I can sense it in their scrunched up eyes and shaking bodies, as they pray for a good death. And Ganga, their mother, the great storyteller, the one they call the compassionate goddess, laughs. She laughs with mirth as she tells me of the anguished death seekers of Kashi, even as her waters lap around them, caressing their skins, even as she accepts the flowers they reverentially drop into her bosom. She weaves such stories in her inimitable way that I am forced to laughter despite myself. Then I am quickly moved to pity as I watch the endless procession that wades into her with such hope. I know their pleas fall on deaf ears.

But I have a secret if only they would listen, could listen to me, if they could tune out her magnificent presence and pay some attention to me. I want to tell them that it takes patience and a special appreciation of quietness to listen to me. But few mortals have the talent or desire for these qualities. If they could just look beyond Ganga's golden beauty and gaze upon my cool silver-green flow their fears might be eased. But they do not look my way for I am the afterthought goddess, the less powerful one, the not-so-glorious Yamuna. I feel sorry for them for I have the best secret of all.

Death is my beloved brother, Lord Yama, king of that otherworld, the thought of whom makes people freeze with terror. Both of us are children of the sun. My brother has given me a power that makes even Ganga jealous, perhaps just one of the reasons she tries to outshine me in every other way. I have a gift in which lies the redemption of mankind. I am Yamuna, remover of the fear of death. Within my healing waters lies the power to relieve you of this eternal burden you carry. Bathe within me, concentrate with pure intent, and you can live your life without looking over your shoulder for my brother, without forever fearing his arrival. Even as his shadow falls upon you, even as you hear the snorts of the fearsome bull he rides upon, even as you spy the golden mace and noose he carries, you will smile. You have already won over him, you have vanquished Lord Yama, because his greatest weapon is your fear.

Ganga's waters once washed the feet of Lord Vishnu, which sanctified her forever. But I, I was his witness, protector and playmate, his silent partner; when incarnated as Lord Krishna he frolicked within me. Still I hear the plaintive, beautiful cry of his flute, a melodic current floating on the evening breeze and I feel his hands slip between my waves and caress my beating heart.

I am a hundred times holier than Ganga though most mortals do not know this, for this knowledge too is my secret. And like all secrets you must work at it, untying tiny knots of mysteries until all is unravelled and laid bare. Secrets are not stories, available for all to see. No, they are treasures to be savoured and discovered by those who can slip under the surface and find the kernel of spotless truth.

I know secrets about this girl who sleeps so soundly on my banks, this victim of Ganga. As she touches my rippling surface, I reach out and soothe her pains and torments and let my waters salve the wounds she makes upon her body. Ganga had told me about this mad seeker. She chuckled as she described her insanity and her anguish.

This girl does not fully trust me, for I am too closely linked by ties of family with Ganga. I knew the exact moment when my voice wrapped around her, when she finally heard me, for I have been patiently calling to her since her arrival in this city. I am sure that she was waiting for me. Or at least a part of her was.

This night when her fears float on the surface, scraped raw and bleeding, as she contemplates another change in her life, as she becomes unneeded, she has left herself open. I see my opportunity and flow in, trying to brush up against the hurting places within her, washing away her fears, even if just for tonight.

Tonight she sleeps, unmolested by her nightmares, though she cries still as she dreams of her happier past, and battles with the realization that it is time once again to move on. Her salty tears flow into me, just as my waters had entered her, and I am touched. I am saddened for her. We come together, becoming one with a whispered sigh.

I know all too well the agony of losing family and home because I too am a refugee from another world and another time. I too lost my home through no fault of my own. Are you ready to hear more secrets about me? To know me? To truly know me? Shhh… shhhh… shhh… focus, concentrate on the gentle kissing sounds of my waves as they brush against the sandy shores, and listen to my most precious, most important secret.

Once I was known as Yami, a child living happily with my twin, Yama, and with my father, the glorious Surya and my mother,

Sanjana, the goddess of consciousness. Sanjana is the force who makes people aware of who they are deep inside. She makes them understand their selves, the good and the bad and every aspect in between. You might know my mother by another name, however, for she has many. At some places, she is worshipped as Bhagirathi, named after the mortal who begged her to come down from heaven and flow upon the earth. Of course, you will know her best as Ganga, the eternal mother, the redeemer of sin and the refuge of the dead.

She had married my father, that eternal charioteer, the most powerful force in the universe, he who embodies the timeless trinity, for she had been dazzled by him like everyone else. In the morning he is Brahma, the creator, bringing to the world the new, child-like morning when everything and anything is possible. During the day he blazes upon the earth as Vishnu, the most powerful god of all, the one who keeps all creation as it is. He rules over time, keeping everything in balance. At night, he is subsumed into the dark presence of Shiva, the virile destroyer in whose mysterious folds the world rests with weariness.

I could talk about my father forever, for I love him, but let me tell you about my mother instead. She is fickle and proud, though as a child I adored her exciting, golden presence in my life. I loved her. We were happy, all four of us, living as a family. Until one day, she decided she could bear my father's intensity no longer. He exhausted her. Our life together bored her. So, she left him and us, like a coward and a trickster. She created a shadow of herself, Chhaya, and left her behind to fool us so that we might never know of her desertion.

Chhaya, who was an exact replica of my mother, bore other children with our father as time went on. Soon she started to treat us like the stepchildren that we were. Lost and frightened we clamoured to know what had changed our mother so drastically, what had become of the one we remembered with such love and we resolved to complain about her to father when he returned that night. She discovered our plans. So she cursed us, the children of the all-powerful sun, while he was away, changing our existence in an instant.

She cursed my gentle brother making him a chandal, one who exists in the dreaded, unclean company of the dead, and sent him to the otherworld. He lives there as its lord, trapped forever in the nether regions of darkness and pain. She cursed my quick, honest tongue and turned me into this flowing and eternal river, and here I am, destined to flow forever.

Chhaya may have been just a shadow, but to me she will forever be the true reflection, the essence of my mother who rampages through the lives of others as if they are of no consequence. For to her, they are not.

And what of this girl? Her secrets eat away at her, burrowing from the inside out, making her evaluate and re-evaluate the life she seeks. She killed her lover, the man who protected her, who took nothing from her that she was not ready to give. She plunged her knife into his body and took away his life because she was lost, weakened by Ganga's evil suggestions, which seemed to come from within her own self and from which there was no escape.

Despite her best devices, she had become attached again, to Nafasat Bai and her incarnations and the house that had been her home in Agra. She was needed, maybe even indispensable for a while, for she saved a life, perhaps as recompense for the one she had taken in Kashi. And now those threads, those connections are unravelling. Chhappan Bai is transformed once again, into Andaliib, and Nadee is cut loose, adrift, with no direction, nowhere to go.

These are the secrets she carries close to her breast, where they nestle against the remains of her life. There are some secrets she tells no one, no, not even me. Some of them I can discern because I am patient and because she has poured them out through the salt water that washes from her eyes and mixes with my waves.

I have another secret: a fear, really. That this girl, this person who calls herself Nadee, is beyond me. Beyond my powers of help. She has no real fear of death and of loss, for she has already borne those. How can she fear the loss of things she does not have? She has secrets and desires that are too fragile and unspoken, gossamer cobwebs that flutter in the recesses of her soul. And even I, patient goddess, remover of fears, cannot hope to wash them away forever.

There are some secrets too powerful for me to battle with, too deep for me to reach.

Instead, I sing to her sweet lullabies and draw her into sleep. I use my powers to leach out her fears, transforming her nightmares into dreams, her unrestful sleep into relaxing slumber.

It is temporary, this rest. When she wakes up she will again be drawn into the ruins of her existence. Till then, sleep, Nadee. Sleep without fear. Sleep…

11

Invisible

The sounds of rain: tiny drums beating on the roof, liquid melodies, roaring thunder, seep into my consciousness one drop at a time. They steal under my eyelids, straining themselves, drop by drop, into my brain, until gradually I come awake and realize that another monsoon has crept upon me. An old dread spreads its night-wings upon my soul, beating a tattoo of terror upon my heart.

I am protected, high up, in the fort, but still if I close my eyes I am trapped within the strong swirls of a river, feeling the lash of the rain in a world enraged, the salt-rusty taste of my own blood upon my tongue.

I repeat a chant of safety, willing my heartbeat to slow. My endless fears make me tremble and I wrap my arms around myself, warming myself from the inside out.

This night I lie awake and gaze into the cloud-darkened sky, through the curtains, trying to make my way through millions of possibilities and reasons. I probe emotions that lie beneath my suffocating armour, breeding thoughts and fears that evaporate only at daybreak. At the core of the noise in this sleepless city of Agra beats a heart of silence, within me, a small centre of stillness in the the tumult, that just a short distance away is being chewed and spat out.

Agra has been a restless city for a while, preparing itself for the move to Fatehpur-Sikri, a process that will take years. Workers from all over the kingdom have been gathered and sent to the new city, in stages. Sikri, the little stonecutters' village, is being transformed into a grand city, with magnificent structures that will house the seat of power. The city is growing, surrounding the original, humble village. Courtiers and noblemen leave Agra as soon as their new homes are completed. An entire city of men is forced to work day and night, to facilitate everything. Our time of departure draws close and despite its inevitable place in my destiny I struggle with my doubts.

I have become too used to Agra. It is a city, which from behind the walls of the fort is much different from the one I used to watch from my little window in the house of courtesans. This Agra thrums with energy, intrigue and power and I feel out of step with it, as if I am an observer trapped between two panes of glass, unable to move, unwilling to look away. Sometimes I venture into the market place and visit the old house but I am a polite stranger at both places, without a role or a place. I know my mad reputation fills them all with unease. Sometimes I am unable to maintain the pretence of sanity and beg them to help me search for my life. I find their looks of horror amusing and when I start laughing I stop only when my eyes fill with tears as I begin to cry.

~

Andaliib-e-Jahan is now part of the court of Emperor Akbar and I am an insignificant member of her entourage. I rarely see her, attended as she is by her new, court-versed glamorous servants who wait on her every whim. On the few occasions that we run into each other she turns her face away as if seeing me reminds her too much of her past, her mistakes, her lost beauty, those months of dependence upon me and of her pain. Perhaps my presence makes her think too much of who she used to be.

I find it hard to believe that I had sat across from her in the palanquin that had delivered her to the fort, watching her hands twist against each other in her lap even as she smiled to herself. It took the loss of love and looks and fifty-six knife wounds to bring her to this. I know both she and I had once wondered if this reward had made her ordeal and re-emergence worthwhile. She would never have to live in a house of courtesans again, never be called a woman of easy virtue. She had found respectability, the only kind she could have ever hoped to achieve. She could practise her art, live with some independence and be an entertainer, a performer for royalty.

She has an apartment of her own – granted it is not as grand as those in which the women of the royal household live, and yes, it is not even in the same compound as them, but it is a home and it is her own. It has been given to her, along with the servants, and all the clothes and jewellery she could ever want and the title that proclaims her new place in the world.

Tall, thick walls separate us from the other sections of the fort. I do not need to strain to hear the sounds of feminine laughter, the low hum of conversation, and children's cries and know that the zenana, the women's quarters lie somewhere beyond these walls. That is a respectable world, guarded and unbreachable, that neither Andaliib nor I can ever hope to enter. To do so would be to step over several demarcating lines in these worlds within worlds and I recognize the echoes of my time at Kashi: thoughts of another wall and other sounds that informed me of my exclusion from someone's life.

I am perfecting the delicate art of becoming invisible, of becoming a ghost that lurks in shadows. I do this because my foreknowledge tells me this path leads to my salvation. I gingerly touch the mementos of my past so as not to tear the old cloth, and take myself to a place where I really do not exist.

Speak, if at all, in a low volume, and perhaps listeners will convince themselves it was just the sound of the wind. Walk slowly, always a step behind the crowd, yet not separate, and you will cease to be a part of it. Never laugh when others can hear you… laughter is the surest presence of life and the bane of invisibility. Cry softly, always at night, when you cannot be seen, even if you weep with your eyes open and your tears saturate your sheets. These are the ingredients of invisibility, its magic potion, and I am perfecting it, making it an art form.

My hair is no longer wild and I keep my eyes downcast, hiding my true self lest someone glimpse the beast that lives within me and divines the quest that drives me, the secrets that agitate at a low simmer. I speak softly and in short sentences until I feel my mind collapsing under the accumulated words that I have storehoused, instead of speaking them out aloud. I rarely attend any of the activities that make the fort hum with excitement every night. These huge gatherings, when Andaliib sings for the emperor, are affairs that can go on all evening and into the night. The emperor, it seems, cannot get enough of her voice and sometimes exhorts her to sing with Mian Tansen, whose voice, it is said, can light lamps by its magnificent power, then summon rain-clouds to extinguish the flames. When they sing together I cannot escape their voices that soar into the skies and spread into the inner reaches of the fort.

I sit in my room and listen to their mingled voices rise into the night, as one. Hers full of the sweet pain that is love and his overflowing with the wisdom of the ages, shot through with mature passion and unfulfilled longing. I listen to their duets without seeing them and they become mere voices, the people behind them as invisible as I am. I smile to myself when I think of such things.

Invisibility is a secret weapon, just as madness is. Madness keeps people at a distance, scaring them, repelling them from coming closer. Invisibility takes me and my madness underground, hidden and secretive, a weapon wrapped within a weapon. Someone might breach one defence but not both.

I have a room of my own, round with many latticed windows, the top floor of Andaliib's apartment, fluttering curtains blowing this way and that in the wind. I am the only one of her servants who has her own room, perhaps because of her lingering sense of gratitude, or perhaps because no one wants to share space with me. It really does not matter. Her little home abuts the wall of the fort and I spend most of my time walking on the walls that two elephants can stand on side by side. The solid strength of the walls under me comforts me and holds me back. I often wonder what it would be like to just step off into empty air.

I am sure Yamuna would catch me and take me away, and I would be buoyed by her strong currents to begin a journey different from the one for which I am destined. I sit at the edge of the wall and dangle my legs freely, leaning back on my hands until they begin to ache and tremble under the strain of supporting the full weight of my body. Yamuna's calm presence and intoxicating whispers are my only refuge within these walls.

Far beneath me flows Yamuna and this is where we commune. She has told me many secrets that sound strangely familiar, as if I had heard them somewhere, perhaps in my now-distant childhood or in my journey to Agra. Irritated with the gaps in my memory I strike my head repeatedly as I try to jar something into place but I cannot remember. I give up and give in to Yamuna's soothing whispers as she tells me her multi-layered secrets, dense with meaning and fragile in their unstable liquidness. Perhaps if I can unravel all of Yamuna's secrets I will find my life that lies scattered and separated somewhere away from me. She has given me peace of a kind for short spaces of time, and I am thankful. I have not slept this well in months and though my dreams are unabated and terrifying she makes me forget them by morning, so I awaken refreshed. But she has not been able to make me forget about my past. I know what my future will bring and I live my present, but my past, my life, remains an elusive ghostly quest.

I wonder what my life would have been, what it was and what it is. I have stopped trying to recreate the face of my dead husband and my phantom children have faded away into whispers and hazy dreams. I do remember my parents still, but they too are disintegrating into things said and left unsaid, less human and more memories. The only presence who remains entrenched in my life is the Dom Raja and I cling to his memory fiercely, reluctant to let it go.

Agra is a city possessed, as preparations for the creation of the new city gather momentum. The emperor is mostly away on his war campaigns and hunting trips but he too is possessed, bent on the creation of his new capital that will celebrate his victory and venerate the man, the saint who brought hope to his life and kingdom.

Andaliib spends most of her time waiting, even more so than she had in the old house, where she had nightly performances. For despite her grand title she is just one of the hundreds of musicians and entertainers who form this court and they all await the emperor's pleasure. She is his favourite performer of the moment, but still most of her time is spent doing nothing while he wages campaigns which take him away from the fort for months at a time, and the affairs of state that occupy him when he is in Agra. She and the other performers wait to perform at short notice when his court is in session, and then only when the evening winds down. So she sleeps, writes poetry and spends time gossiping with the other female entertainers, sometimes playing chaupar or other board games with them.

It is as if by reaching her ultimate goal of leaving the house – and surpassing it - she is at a loose end, unsure of what to do. I wonder often if she still dreams of her dead lover. Can she feel his kisses, his hands gliding slowly upon her body as I can still feel the Dom Raja? Does he come to her in the dead of night, with silent footsteps, the knife glinting in his hands with which he cuts her heart into shreds before he claims her as his own, forever?

When I was a child, running away from my mother's swift slaps and my many chores, I just wanted to sit and be still, to think of my future. Once I told my mother that I wanted to find a place of comfort where I could do nothing all day, which made her laugh, for such a desire was unthinkable and way outside my parent's realm of expectation or knowing. She had told me that I could only gain my heart's desire if I lived in the emperor's palace. Perhaps even then I knew that one day I would achieve my goal of doing nothing for this is what I do all day here. And my mind races with my heart as I make up things to do.

I exchange secrets with Yamuna and wander around the fort, trying to make time stand still in small moments for that, I am convinced, is crucial for true invisibility, and that is the only trick I work on. I spend hours looking at one drop of water that I place on one small leaf and examine the tiny shifting rainbows within it, the light that trembles on it, its perfect roundness, its indescribable colour.

I lie on my back on the ramparts and look at the sky until it blurs into a blue expanse within my eyes. I wonder when and if someone will notice that I have not spoken for days. I know that in this bustling city within a city there could be fifty wandering, wilfully mute women and no one would notice. I speak only to

Yamuna and that too not in words, for she and I have worked out a language all our own.

~

The rain intensifies and the darkness is pierced by occasional blazing arrows of lightning. I huddle under my bedclothes, stuffing my fingers into my ears, and remember another lonely night like this, on the way from Kashi to Agra. I do not want to remember but my thoughts are out of my control. I must remember. The rain makes me remember.

It had been several days since I had fled the city of the dead. I awakened in the depth of one starless night, feeling a strange stickiness on my hands. I licked my palm to try and discern the substance from its taste. The thick, gagging, metallic-sourness of blood made my eyes come open. In the flickering flashes of the jagged seams of lightning that were ripping the sky apart, I could see the brightness of red on my palms, a parody of the red bridal henna that had never adorned them.

Then I felt him lie down beside me in the dark and I froze. How could this be? His body warm, his breath warmer still, stirring the little hairs that stand guard at my hairline, his hands callous-rough yet gentle as they rove over me. This cannot be. No, no… it cannot be. I open my eyes fully trying to see, trying to tear through the darkness and see the reality, but the night was absolute, inside this little room in the corner of one of the emperor's many inns.

I knew then, that no matter how far I went I could never escape him, would never want to escape him. The strong sun of the day might keep him away but at night, when the unconscious emerges, he would always return. To me. The thought is equal parts dread, acceptance and comfort. I fall asleep as his kiss falls on my brow. I remember that night with inevitability. I remember it with excitement. I remember because I cannot forget. I remember because he comes to me still.

All the time I was at the house, tending to the woman who was to be Andaliib, he had stayed away except in my dreams. As if he knew and I knew that the veils of reality would keep him away from me. But tonight as the rain thunders overhead and lightning bolts pierce the sky, I feel my heart thud inside me, leaping inside my chest with fright. Then I feel him again, like a sigh upon my skin. I feel his kiss below my left breast where I have marked a space for him. My fingers retrace the path of his lips. My breathing slows, my lids are weighted and I drift into a state in which Yamuna's lullabies comfortingly mingle with his touch. I sleep.

Dawn brings with it preparations for the move. Fatehpur-Sikri is not yet completed but the section allocated to the entertainers is ready to receive us. The emperor awaits us there, eager to listen to Andaliib's songs, hoping to soothe his travel fatigue.

We trace the path of Yamuna for a distance, the sway of the elephant under me drawing me into a hypnotic state. The river tells me her secrets and I tell her mine and for a moment we are best friends, one with each other, glimpsing our own hidden realities in one another. She is trying to tell me something through her secrets, something that I cannot fully comprehend. I listen.

'You are leaving me today but you carry me with you still, with all your secrets, for in each one there is a drop of me,' she says in a liquid-silver trill of laughter.

It is true. I am leaving Agra and going to a place where there is no river. I am bereft. To whom will I tell my secrets? Who will want to listen? Who will make me their secret confidante? I have perfected the art of being invisible to such a degree that people do not even realize I am in their presence.

Fears pound into my brain, like a merciless hailstorm, obliterating all other thoughts. Agra had become home to me. Its winding streets and broad avenues, its houses – all gracious arches and pillars – the river flowing on one side, the energy of a capital city, the sounds of the streets that never died away. It had all become familiar. And now I must leave.

Zameerpur, the cradle of my childhood, is fast becoming a hazy memory and Kashi remains too involved with death, but Agra is dizzying, exciting life, the centre of the world and I had found a place in it, however transitory and flimsy it had been.

Now I am adrift again, as our caravan makes a turn away from the river, my only true friend. I turn to look back as the elephant under me moves slowly, its movements languorous, like a beautiful and lazy woman. Yamuna's waters reflect the sun and sparkle like silver bells, just for an instant. Then we turn again and she is lost in the distance, a slender thread that merges into a distant mirage. One last time, however, she wraps her liquid presence around me as she sighs, 'farewell'. I let out the breath I have been holding as I close my eyes and confide in her, tell her a final secret. A precious truth. I cannot hear her answer, but I know she has heard me.

12

Secret Victories

The glory of battles is celebrated far away from the bloody, limb-strewn, fields where men unleash terrible atrocities on one another. Victory is only recognized when the roar of cannons no longer thunders, when the ground no longer shakes under the assault of an army of elephants, when death does not come swiftly on horseback or borne on the deadly songs of arrows that whistle in the wind. War is celebrated through elaborate verses that eulogize the valour of the dead and of the victorious, that diminish and trample over the remains of the dead and defeated. Victories are venerated and preserved forever, crystallized in time through mighty monuments that rise to meet the sky, proclaiming the triumph for centuries, preserving it for history and posterity.

A gate is being built now at Fatehpur-Sikri, which stands proudly facing the newly-conquered western territories. The Buland Darwaza, the tallest gate in the land, is as its name suggests a portal that scales proud heights, a regal and indomitable reminder of defeat to the vanquished enemy, an implacable symbol of victory.

Ornate calligraphy in black marble is inlaid into the red sandstone that arches high overhead:

Jesus, Son of Mary (on whom be peace) said: The World is a Bridge, pass over it, but build no houses upon it. He, who hopes for a day, may hope for eternity; but the World endures but an hour. Spend it in prayer, for the rest is unseen.

Entrance into the emperor's city of victory is gained by passing under this mighty gate. It is an entrance to plush royalty, implacably planted upon silent rivers of blood and it speaks of the impermanent state that is this worldly life. I read the inscription often, for it makes me smile as I ponder its ironic meaning.

~

In this new capital of the kingdom dust dances like whirling dervishes, tiny razor-sharp particles that clog my nose and settle into each pore of my skin. The land has been carved into rough crags, scrubby bushes hanging on to them with dogged determination. The rains that usually drench Agra barely touch down here. Whenever they do arrive, however, the pounding showers gouge out the dry, thirsty soil, reshaping the landscape, washing away the dry dust and the deeper earth, making cultivation almost impossible. It is a shape-shifting world in which the land patiently battles the onslaught of water, wind, sun and lightning.

Sounds of construction travel on unabated waves until, after a few months, they have merged into the background and can be heard no longer. The city and the fort continue to be built around us and its din will echo and re-echo in Fatehpur-Sikri for years to come. Red sandstone and white marble dust mingle with the sand particles that whirl in the air, coating everything and everyone in multicoloured cloaks. Workers, artists and artisans labour to create a city of dreams for a visionary emperor, a city that the world has never seen nor is likely to. Buildings, sprung from fertile imaginations, are being hewn, chiselled and tapped into existence. Fantastic sculptures and frescoes depicting lavish winged beings and lush gardens of paradise are being etched into stone walls, where they will frolic in their frozen state for centuries.

The fort is being constructed on a hill, the ramparts falling away into the brown-baked ravines below. At a distance from the fort, away from the old village of Sikri, the common people, the merchants and the support staff who arrive each day from Agra, are building their own homes. These are humble dwellings, built of the native rock, their rooms small and close together, giving them an aura of community.

The emperor is also having constructed an inn for the weary travellers of his vast kingdom. Its many domes and two storeys of rooms can house several hundred humans and their animals at any given time. The tiny chambers are arranged in a square and in the centre is a huge courtyard. This courtyard is where travellers will gather to cook, talk and exchange news by the red flames of their flickering fires. For now, however, all we can see and hear is the commotion of construction.

~

Nights in Fatehpur-Sikri fall with dramatic suddenness. It is as if a curtain falls, a curtain shot through with bright, brocade stars. Nightfall here always fills me with disquiet, as if it deliberately sneaks up on me without warning, just to unsettle me. Sometimes I play a waiting game with it, trying to predict the exact moment when the setting sun's last rays will be erased by the rolling sigh of night. I wait, hand tensed, a chalk clutched in it, ready to mark the symbol of the quarter moon, upon the broad flagstones in the courtyard the instant of its descent. I have won this game just a few times and I think I will have enough time to master it. Yes… yes, I am sure I will be here long enough to win this game. I will make this place home.

Along with Andaliib's other servants I do my chores and try to stay busy. I steer away from their incessant chatter, their flirtations and their love affairs. Andaliib and I see each other less and less and when we do, I cannot stop my thoughts from turning again to those longs nights when we eavesdropped on each other's nightmares and let our breathing calm each other into eventual sleep. Her blood had once coated my body until I knew not if it was her who bled or I. We were as twins, indistinguishable from one another; now we are strangers playing roles. Mistress and servant.

She treats me with detached, indulgent kindness, just as she had before her transformation, but now her eyes skim over me as if I have retreated into the distant echoes of her life. I wonder sometimes, if her dead nawab has also been relegated into some deep, dark dungeon of her mind. Who else lives there, within her? The nawab, trapped in his eternal agony of love, and I brush against each other like shadows at dusk, each unaware of the other, unknowing of the others who lurk within the undiscovered regions of her self.

There are times, in that moment before her gaze skitters away from me, that I want to ask her, 'Do you think of him still? Do you love him, even now, despite what he did to you? Who have you become? Who am I? Do you remember me? I saved your life… we were the same. Do you… can you remember? We are not strangers, you and I.' The words fall between the spaces of my mind and settle comfortably into the gap between my brain and my tongue. I remain silent in her presence and she never gives me an opportunity to venture above my station.

This new incarnation, not really Nafasat and not quite Chhappan, is a mystery to me. I do not know the impact of the memories she carries, or what she feels, how she thinks and what I am to her. By the healing of her body and the weight of her new and envied status, a door that had stood ajar between us once is closing. Soon it will have been slammed shut decisively and forever, isolating me from her. I know she has new lovers, men enraptured by her blinding talent and dazzling voice; men with the imagination to look beyond her grotesque appearance. A new insatiable and voracious appetite has opened up within her and she tires of her conquests easily, looking for something within them that none of them possess. I hear stories of her wild quests as she uses bodies and emotions, before tossing them aside, without a backward glance as if to say, 'There is nothing from you that I want. Even I, in my monstrous state realize that.' I observe all this from a respectful distance and know that Andaliib is losing herself and the memories of her lost love even as she tries desperately to find both.

We have diverged here, in this place, at this time, and we will never truly meet again. This realization fills me with an angry sadness. Andaliib has been swept up by a powerful force that is larger than all her dammed up emotions and she has pushed me away like a bit of flotsam. I make her remember. In my presence she cannot be truly Andaliib for we are bound by bonds of shared history. I knew her when she writhed in anguish; now, she desires to kill her past and move beyond it. For me she will always be

Chhappan Bai, peerless courtesan who had transcended herself. Her face reminds me of a long-ago friend. She shares a voice with someone I knew once.

~

I have my memories and my secrets and they shall never abandon me, though the pink of the silk has become light, almost white; a shadow of the original colour and the cloth itself is frayed and fragile. Where it is folded the material is starting to disintegrate and I force myself to be careful though I long to press it close to my face and inhale the fading scent of my memories, my lost life. The gold nosering shines with its usual lustre and as I caress it, I feel a pulsing warmth and I wonder if the heat from my mother's hand is still trapped within the metal. The central vein of the feather is brittle and as I feel it gingerly I am afraid of snapping it into many pieces. I close my eyes as I gently touch the silky skeins that flutter in the slight breeze. For an instant, I can feel the sweet easterly wind that blew into Zameerpur at the beginning of each summer. The wind plays with a lock of my hair. I smile.

I have unwrapped my bundle with care, in a protected corner, not wanting the eyes of others to intrude upon the tattered remains of who I once was. My hand snakes up my shirt and I rest my cool palm against the warm place under my breast where my fingers trace the deep indentation. I feel the energy of his presence wash over me. Using the rhythmic beats of my heart that flutter against my palm, he is sending me a message that I am only now beginning to decode. Gradually my hand is warmed by the heat from my body and I realize something I have already known. The knowledge comes upon me softly, gently, and it is as familiar as the breath that comes from between my lips.

~

He is not dead. He tricked me by stiffening his body and controlling the spurting flow of his blood because despite himself he wanted me to be free. He could not bring himself to say it but he loved me enough to let me leave, forcing me to take the final, determining step. That was the only gift he could give me at the time, freedom through his supposed death. The Dom Raja is alive. That can be the only explanation for this strange quickening within me, the feeling of his presence, his nightly visitations. He did love me. He loves me still.

My heart beats out a message to me from him, 'I am here. I have left everything… everyone for you. I am here. I am here. I am here.'

Everyone else in my life has moved on or been snatched away and I am comforted to know that he remains with me. I had whispered this secret wish to Yamuna before leaving Agra and she had sighed wearily in response, as if tired of my imaginings. But this is not my imagination, he tells me. I feel him. I know him. He is here. With me.

~

Sheikh Salim Chishti is a part of Fatehpur forever. Even his death cannot erase that. He is a palpable, tangible force, very much alive for those who seek him. I have heard stories that he could look not only into the uncertain future, but he could also change it as he had demonstrated to the emperor. In blessing the throne of Hindustan with an heir and two younger princes, he had displayed his powers and secured for himself a place in history. I wonder how he lived with this burden of knowing, how he survived, without his mind buckling, crumbling under the pressure. I want to learn his secret.

Now that his magnificent new tomb is being created, a jewel box of marble and inlaid gems, his austere cave is no longer the destination for those asking for his blessings, begging for their wishes to be fulfilled. They are starting to visit the half-completed tomb that stands in the huge courtyard of the largest mosque in the country, entering through the Buland Darwaza, where the emperor himself leads the faithful in prayer.

The path leading to his old grotto, where he meditated and spent many nights and days, is hard packed, the soil held together by the rough vegetation and the roots of the few trees which have managed to withstand the ravages of time and weather. The path has just recently fallen into disuse and is being reclaimed by the hardy plants and bushes that flourish there now.

Still, someone, some loyal devotee, keeps a lamp lit in the dark cave. The lamp is dying as I walk in, its spluttering flames throwing fantastic shadows on the uneven surfaces of its walls. His mat still lies on the floor as if he will walk in any moment, caught up in the Sufi junoon – the passionate madness – that allows for total immersion in communication with God. They say Sheikh Chishti has never left Sikri, the village that was his earthly home. His divine presence dwells on in this land and these rocks, in this village where he lived. They are right.

As the flame dies away, a thin plume of smoke drifts toward me, like a dying breath. The mouth of the cave becomes indistinguishable from the darkness outside. The din from the fort is muted and manageable, an annoying hum that does not fully penetrate into me here.

I sit cross-legged on his mat, feeling a peace soak into me that I have never felt before, not even in Yamuna's presence, not even when I lived in Zameerpur. He has not been dead for long and I can still smell the scent of his life on the rough material. He is the granter of wishes, the open conduit to the heavens, a dervish who laid himself open to commoners and emperors alike. I want nothing from him. I have no wishes I need to be granted. I want him to be my confessor, my silent confidante this one night. So I tell him all.

I tell him of the Dom Raja's miraculous re-entry into my life; of the sloughing away of my burgeoning, awakened guilt like it was dead skin. I tell him of my lover's visits to me, late at night, when I am transported away from this world, of the agonizing ecstasy I feel in his presence in the absolute dark.

And then I tell him of the secret, the biggest secret of all that lives within me and grows each day. I had not been able to confide it to Yamuna because it had seemed so impossible, so improbable, even to me. For that was before I had become certain that the Dom Raja was truly alive, that I was not in the grip of a never-ending nightmare. And now, for once in a long time, something makes sense, falling into a place in my mind.

I smile as I tell him what I know.. The sounds from the outside world fade away and the moon sails behind a cloud in the black-purple sky, its light blanked out for a long moment. This cave, at the edge of the city of victory, has for now, become the centre of my universe, the repository of my most nurtured secret. Something that is the culmination of the emptiness that has gnawed at me, for that is now going to be obliterated forever.

From its place over my heart, my hand moves to caress my stomach, slowly, as I allow myself to say the words out aloud. 'He lives within me, a boy child. I will bring him into this world. He will be someone of whom his father is proud. I will love him and nurture him and he will be mine. He is mine.'

The child within me is just the whisper of a dream, a wisp, an insubstantial clot of blood. But soon… soon, he will grow within me and emerge from me, blood of my blood, heart of my heart, soul of my soul.

The moon emerges from its cloud-cover and its light shines upon the land, as if in celestial celebration of the articulation of my secret. I fall asleep on the Sheikh's mat and as my mind edges towards oblivion, I feel my lover settle in beside me as he whispers into my ear, 'I am here.' His whisper curves around me like a velvet shroud and I smile sleepily before giving in to a deep rest.

13

Child of Dreams

I see a pearl. It is perfect, round and pinkish-white, like the first blush of dawn, and it glistens like a large tear on my palm, absorbing all available light, trapping it within itself. With a slow burst it collapses, transforming into a single, fragile drop of water that I carry with me down, down to the depths where the tendrils of the water hyacinth float in a slow dance. I close my hand around the precious pearl, not willing to let it get away from me, aware of its importance, knowing that it represented all that I had lost. As I work to free myself, all the trapped voices of my past call to me.

I hold the water-pearl in one hand. As I look down at it, my hand and arm gleam white like bone, as if the water had bleached all the colour out of my skin, leaving it a pale ghost. Alarmed, I open my hand and watch helplessly as the gem falls away from me, swirling further down into the surrounding murkiness. Panicked, I dive down into the dark depths. It becomes impossible for me to see anything, not even my own hand in front of me. All that is left are those soft voices calling my name.

I awake slowly, keeping my eyes closed, as if by doing so I could hold on, could continue listening to those fading voices, holding them close to me. Of late I have begun to wonder about these voices. Do they beg me to untangle them or are they calling me to them, hoping that the giant tendrils will trap me, keeping me with them forever? Perhaps, one night I will fight not to awaken, give in, and never return to the land of not-dreams on the surface. Instead I shall live in my dreamscape, forever, with all the people from my past, in a reality that will never change. I come fully awake with only the Dom Raja's voice ringing in my ears, feeling his warmth next to my body, his kiss upon my brow.

~

Paradise is a vision of cascading water flowing into carefully crafted lakes and stylized, lush-flowing rivers of life; it is glorious flowers and trees in various shades of washed, vivid green. Paradise is laid out in an intricate grid that beckons spirituality with its ordered beauty. It calls to itself those who are tired of the chaos and uncertainty of their daily lives. Paradise is glimpsed in these elaborate gardens created by a people, who just a generation ago, were nomads and whose only quest was to escape the privations of a harsh and dusty life. Visions of paradise imparted dreams of everlasting life when death was but a footstep away. Paradise is an oasis of beauty in the dry, desert-like landscape of Fatehpur-Sikri, recreated by the emperor of Hindustan.

Interspersed between the many palaces, administrative structures and public buildings of Fatehpur-Sikri are these garden idylls: serenely beautiful, they invoke visions of the eternal rest and beauty promised to the faithful. It is easy for me to get lost in them, and I do that often.

I lie under a tree, watching its fronds swish gently in the breeze, the movement of the air fanning my cheeks as I talk to the Dom Raja through the child that stirs within me. They are inextricably linked, father and son – they are now both bound to me for all time. The moon is full tonight and it is suspended above my head, so close that I can see its every imperfection, each dark scar on its surface. The monthly rhythm of the moon tugs at my body, aligning me with its journey across the night skies. I feel its powerful pull, tugging at something within me, different somehow tonight than it has been at any other time. The moon's passage marks the time in intervals until my son is born. Each full moon I can tell that his body within me has grown some more, that the person he is to be is being formed more fully. I smile at this secret relationship between the silver timekeeper in the sky and me.

Perhaps my dream child smiles too. He is still a flutter under my heart, an incomplete emotion, an unclear hope, an indistinct human and I love him fiercely. I tell him of the world he will come into and I whisper to him secrets about his father and me.

My child, you were conceived with love, on a dark, dark night when the sky was blanketed with clouds and the earth stood still. You will take on the mantle of your father's power and you will recognize its place in your life. You will not be invisible like me. You will grow up brave, unafraid and the world shall take notice of your existence. Can you feel my caress? Can you feel my love through the layers of skin and flesh that still separate us? Soon I will hold you in my arms and I shall never be alone. You are all my hopes, my dreams, my unsaid desires. You are mine.

~

Some evenings I venture outside the walls of the fort, slipping out unnoticed, like a shadow. There is a body of water at the bottom of the ravine. Fatehpur Lake is a sheet of liquid that shimmers and shakes with ripples and tiny waves. It seems unnatural somehow, that this vast expanse of water is trapped by seams of brown earth, contained forever within this finite space. I feel sad for this water that has never experienced and never will, the joy of flowing through icy mountains and verdant green plains on its way to the sea. This lake will never escape its natural limits, it will continue the ebb and flow of its miniature tides within its neatly defined boundaries.

On nights when the trapped heat that blasts the earth still shivers in waves suspended in the air, I dip my feet in the cool water. Even though this lake is mute and trapped unlike the rivers of my past, I talk to her. I tell her of the two great rivers. I tell her secrets and stories and I describe the places she will never see, the sights that she will never experience. Sometimes, it seems, she kisses my feet in gratitude and I stare gently into her depths as I feel my son stir within me.

~

I have been aware for a few days that there is something different about the emperor's city – that something is not quite right. This has penetrated even my consciousness. This feeling is not connected with affairs of state or distant wars. There is a strange buzz of discomfort, a fear perhaps… or is it a sense of wonder? People rush about, talking in hushed tones. But I am too involved with my unborn child to find out what is happening. I am too preoccupied to listen to the nudges from my foreknowledge.

One day I, with Andaliib's other servants, air out the bedding and thoroughly clean her house. We carry out all the mattresses, the sheets, and the curtains and lay them in the strong sunlight, letting the heat kill any lingering germs. One of the giggling girls beats the mattresses with a long stick, raising clouds of fine dust. We wash out the floors, wiping and polishing them until they gleam. Through all of this I am forced to listen to their incessant chatter. Their conversation drifts around me, enfolding me between its many layers. I am intrigued despite myself, this looking into other people's lives, into a world outside of myself.

'I mean, people say he is a great emperor, so why is he so upset over a bauble, however fine?'

'It was a gift from his father. The Emperor Humayun gave it to him when he was but a child… it was a connection with his past. He is heartbroken.'

'Tcch tchhh… yes, they think it must be lost somewhere on the way when he was returning from the last campaign. Who knows where he dropped it? Or who stole it?'

'If someone can find it, that person will be rewarded. I wish I knew where it was.'

'You can't even find yourself a husband, Jamalo. Forget about finding the emperor's treasure, you foolish girl.'

The conversation devolves into a fight. The emperor has lost a link with his past, a symbol of his father, Emperor Humayun who despite being a weak and ineffectual king was a man who loved his son above all.

~

A battle rages in the night, the darkness punched by flashes of light and made more absolute by the glowing bluish haze from the smoke that lingers after the firing of guns and cannons. The smell of gunpowder burns eyes and invades every pore on the bodies of the combatants. The attackers are looking for someone, for the then emperor and his family.

The Emperor Humayun and his young wife are whisked away by faithful soldiers. 'My son… my baby. Where is my son?' the mother cries, as she struggles against her husband's arms that bind her to him with the urgency of escape. Her wails echo in the night, a sound that is lost in the roar of the cannons and blast of muskets and all the gory business of dying and killing.

The young prince's wet nurse hands him over to his uncle, the leader of the advancing army that had stolen upon the nomad, dethroned monarch's camp in the middle of the night. Prince Kamran, brother of Humayun, smiles at his nephew who looks up at him unafraid and curious, before screwing up his face and letting forth a crescendo of cries. 'We know whose son this is. Why would he be glad to see us?' Prince Kamran says.

The baby's flailing hands brush against a sparkling red gem that dangles from a blood-red ribbon around his uncle's neck. Aaaah, what a treasure… a toy. His tears disappear as he grabs the locket in his fat hands, pulling his uncle's face towards him. The man holding him laughs, and taking off the necklace, gives it to the child who is fascinated by his new toy. Prince Akbar passes into the care of his uncle, his father's rival and mortal enemy, one of the two contenders to the throne of Hindustan.

As the baby takes his first steps, his uncle plays the role of his father. He tosses his turban at him, making him fall, thus besting the evil spirits who might harm him out of jealousy. The future emperor of Hindustan lives with his uncle for two years looked after by his nurses and servants. Then he is rescued by faithful soldiers in his father's employ. Before he can be put into his mother's arms, however, he is again spirited away, this time a hostage of his other uncle, Daniyal.

There too, he is treated as a prince, but not with much affection. He is merely a pawn, a ploy to entice his father to his death. As Humayun advances on the fort where his child is held prisoner, he is elated at the thought of the long-awaited reunion. He knows his queen awaits word of the rescue, her arms aching to hold her child close.

'Halt!' The leader of his charging cavalry calls, as his men aim their guns towards the walls of the fort. A small, wriggling body is being held over the ramparts, directly in the path of any incoming arrows or gun and cannon shots. The advancing army retreats without rescuing the tiny hostage.

Humayun then builds alliances and gathers a mighty army, which marches and conquers, advancing into Prince Daniyal's territories. The battles are fierce, the retributions quick and brutal. Despite the emperor's temperate poetic soul he fights for his life and for that of his son and for the future of his empire.

Then one day, after years of fighting, he liberates his son and heir from the clutches of his brothers. Finally, he can wipe away his wife's tears and reunite her with their first-born son, the heir to his hard-won empire.

The child, however, still wears the red gem on a now-faded ribbon around his neck, a symbol of his father's enemy and of his own captivity. The father kisses his son on the brow as he tenderly places him on his lap. He removes the ribbon and puts in its place, a peerless treasure. This treasure comes from a place that neither father nor son has seen, from the depths that can swallow the mighty rivers to which they are accustomed. It is a treasure from the sea, nurtured and grown within a shell, whose beginnings were humble, just a particle of sand. It is a perfect pearl, round and glistening with a glowing inner light, the largest that anyone has ever seen.

'This pearl is your mother's tear. It is your father's hope. Take care of both, my son.'

The young prince lets his father replace the ruby that glowed like a large, shiny drop of blood, with this perfect pearl. As he grew and blossomed under his mother's love and his father's tutelage, for Akbar that ruby now symbolized the betrayal of love and trust. It reminded him of the perfidy of humans and of the long separation from his parents.

After his father's death, he began to keep the ruby close to his person again, pinning it to his turban when he was crowned emperor. It was his reminder not to trust too many people and perhaps a gesture of affection towards his now dead uncle who had once loved him like a son, despite it all. His father's gift, however, nestled close to his heart, growing more precious with every beat of his heart.

His father was betrayed by his own blood, by his brothers who had taken advantage of the deathbed promise given to their father, Babar. Emperor Babar had exhorted Prince Humayun to love his brothers no matter what and to forgive them all their trespasses. And time and again Emperor Humayun had forgiven his brothers despite their sins. In the process he had lost his kingdom, become a helpless refugee and had almost lost his son.

When Chhappan Bai's plaintive song of the betrayal of her fragile human heart had risen into the sky on that evening not so long ago, he knew that the ruby had found its next home. He had felt compelled to give the ruby to her, she who had been even more betrayed by love than he or his father had been. But this event happened only after others had taken place.

It was a well-known fact that Emperor Humayun spent many hours in his library, more a scholar than a warrior, more at home with his books than on the battlefield. One evening, lost within the pages of some literary work he heard the call of the muezzin, calling the faithful to prayer. Not wanting to miss his evening congregation he paid little attention to the steep angles of the steps as he hurried down them on his way to the mosque. His foot slipped and he fell, tumbling down the stone stairs to his death. Mohammad Jalal-ud-din Akbar was barely thirteen years old when he was crowned emperor of a tenuously held-together realm. The responsibilities of those who are born to rule came to him before he had crossed the threshold from child to adult.

He took on a kingdom, a huge household and a harem of female relatives. Battles and wars gained prominence in his life, taking him away from the pursuit of arts and letters that stirred his soul. Through all these challenges he had only one moment each day of pure love and support, when he could shed his cares and become once again a boy. Each night he kissed his father's gift before going to sleep, pushing away for an instant his heavy burdens, his obligations and his legacy.

Now years later, after squashing many rebellions and consolidating his powers, he is the most powerful ruler in the land, a man, a husband and a father. His night time ritual has continued through the years.

Until one night as he rested in his palace, on his return from his last campaign, he noticed the absence of the pearl. It was gone and he did not know where or how. The emperor's hands still restlessly search for the non-existent gem, his fingers longing to touch its perfect, smooth, roundness.

Various versions of this story float around the fort, filling in the gaps of the indistinct vision that had already unfolded within me. Montages of sights and sounds and colours and smells underlined by fear and love and death unfurl with unhurried ease in my mind again. I remember the pearl from my dream and before I can swallow the words that I know are about to emerge past my lips, before I can clap my hands around my mouth and stop the relentless march of my destiny, I say them out aloud 'I know where it is.'

~

'You know where we can find our lost gem?' The emperor's voice is smooth steel cloaked in velvet.

'Yes. It lies inside a silk bag.' My voice is swirling around within my head and feels and sounds like a dream, untouched by reality.

He takes a deep breath before going on patiently.

'So you don't know exactly where it is? Which village? Which town? The name of the person who has it?'

'No,' I respond, ' I don't know a name but I do know who has it.'

There is silence as I look at him. Away from the magnificent halls of private and public audience, where his countenance blazes with regal fire, here he seems smaller somehow, tired, human.

I stand before him in the zenana quarters, in a place, a sanctum where women like Andaliib cannot even dare to enter. Past the valiant Rajput warriors, past the huge eunuchs and then past the female guards and record-keepers who keep this zenana safe from outside eyes, I have been brought into his presence.

Water has been brought up from Fatehpur Lake where it lies trapped within a massive red sandstone tank from where it is circulated as needed to several fountains and channels. These fountains splash the cool water into the darkening evening, their cascades glinting under the light of the emerging stars. Four, narrow, elaborately carved red sandstone bridges span the surface of the tank in a criss-cross fashion. They meet at the large square platform in the centre, which is edged by screen balconies all around. This is where the emperor sits, lying back on the cushions arranged around him.

His wives, concubines and other female members of his household all orient their attention towards him even as they sit or mill about. The mother of his heir, the Empress Jodha Bai, also known as Maryam Zamani or Mary of the World, sits closest to him, glancing at him anxiously when he is not looking at her. I barely notice any of the others except as soft-speaking, colourful presences, some beautiful, some plain. They are a rush of shades and hues, from blue-eyed, light-haired Europeans and Afghans to the earth-toned daughters of the deserts and plains of Hindustan.

Yet I feel another presence, somewhat hidden, someone who looks at me with piercing though vacant eyes, even though I ignore her this evening. The laughter of children playing hide and seek fills the air as surely as the fragrance of the night flowers that wafts around us.

The emperor's fingers restlessly trace the rim of his wine goblet as if they ache to touch something else, something that he has lost and cannot wait to recover. He chooses his words carefully, barely containing his impatience.

'How do we find it then? Will I find it?'

'Yes, you shall but not because you search for it. It shall find you, when it is time.'

I have been brought to him as a soothsayer, one who foretells and advises. The emperor has many such in his employ and they help him run his kingdom, ensuring that all his actions and the fate of his kingdom are auspiciously aligned with the stars and the times. There are some who foretell the future, his and that of his realm.

From the time I uttered my strange words into a gathering silence, I had known an inevitable truth. I was climbing out of my cloak of invisibility and heading into his presence. I am still not sure if I was brought here to help find a lost treasure or if I am purely this evening's entertainment. Perhaps Andaliib's giggling servants are tired of me and want me to invite the emperor's wrath by making promises I cannot hope to keep.

'Her skin is white, like a marriage between alabaster and marble. And she shall return to you the treasure you seek.'

I speak those words and run away from his presence. He lets me leave. Past all the guards, past the playing children, past his artfully arranged queens and concubines, away from the inner world of the zenana, back to the outside gardens.

Such is the power of soothsayers; even mad soothsayers seeking their own lives. Emperors dare not ask them to stop.

Suddenly, in speaking one foolish sentence, I am naked, laid bare for all to see, for all to hear. I try to summon the help of all my magic ingredients of invisibility but they fly from my grasp like running water, leaving me vulnerable to the taunting laughs and whispers that follow me everywhere. Each snigger, each taunt slashes into my insides as surely as my own knife slices into my flesh each night. Until all there is left of me is a throbbing, burning pain from the inside out. There is only one solution, one end to this torment, but even as the thought crosses my mind, my hands move protectively to my stomach where my child nestles under my heart. He weakens my resolve.

14

Marble and Alabaster

All sanctuaries, all escapes save my dreams are lost to me now. These people around me whose presence I had sought to escape can see me and hear me. The scabs from my wounds have been ripped off all at once as if by some giant hand, leaving me writhing in burning agony. Whispers ricochet like arrows of pain, piercing my consciousness, tearing into me with vicious ease. I am no longer invisible. I have done this to myself and I have no defences.

'There she is. Who ever noticed her before?'

'I didn't. Everyone told me to stay away from her because she is insane.'

'Oh yes she is quite crazy. Andaliib Begum feels grateful to her for some reason. That's the only reason she is here. She scares me sometimes.'

'Hai Allah, I thought I was the only one she did that to. Have you seen the way she looks sometimes? Almost as if she will kill someone. Rubbing her stomach and whispering some gibberish to herself. Insane, stupid woman.'

'Yes, and now she thinks she is a soothsayer. Went and talked to the emperor too. Mad and shameless'

'Arrey, I thought the emperor would either get a big laugh out of it... or get rid of her somehow. That's why I had the court informed about what she said. But he is too tender-hearted. He didn't even punish her. Tchh tchhh.'

When they tire of speaking among themselves they seek me out. Until this incident created an uproar in the fort, Andaliib's servants had mostly ignored me even if they had resented my place in her past, the room of my own, the secret history their mistress and I shared. They made fun of me if I happened to be around but they usually left me alone.

Now they call out to me as I pass by, 'Ai, Nadee. Ai marriage of alabaster and marble, here wipe down these floors. They are marble too. Oh,.sorry, but no alabaster. No marriage either.' Their laughter and jeers seep into me, unabated, like an inescapable flood, invading my composure from every angle.

'Hey mad girl, when did you start combing your hair?'

'Aah yes, you looked much prettier with that bird's nest on your head.'

'Tell us again… who will bring the emperor's pearl to him?'

'Yes, yes, tell us. Please tell us.'

Their voices blend and merge into one unceasing chant interspersed with their chuckles and laughter.

'Mad… ha ha ha… Nadee…. crazy…stupid… Mad… Nadee.'

One day as I run away from them, the chant ringing in my ears, I slam into someone. Someone who is unsteady on her feet and falls with a thud, on her back onto the hard floor beside me. It is Andaliib. I gaze at her in silence, as she slowly sits up and looks at me. I have jolted her out of her cultivated posture of indifference towards me. For one brief instant we are no longer strangers. Then the moment falters and dies away. She winces as old aches and new ones assault her crippled body.

'I… I am sorry. Please forgive me. I did not see where I was going.'

'No… no. It is all right…'

She tries to get up and I help her to stand on her feet, apologizing, the words flowing from me in an incoherent stream. She leans heavily on me as she says, 'Do not worry about it. You were obviously in a hurry to get somewhere.' Her voice is kind as always though detached as if trying to convince me and herself that she truly does not recognize me. As if I am just one of her other maidservants. The warmth of her skin radiates into mine as I grasp her weakened right arm to help her up from the floor.

I watch helplessly as a single tear that has rolled down my face splashes upon her bare forearm, where it glistens like a jewel, inset within one of her dark scars. Hurriedly I wipe it off her skin and turn away with a whispered apology. I am not sure if I felt her hand linger on my arm as I wrenched it away. Did she gently squeeze my arm before I hurried away, or was that just my own imagination, born out of my yearning for comfort and contact?

That was the last time the maids made fun of me directly, the last time I heard them talk about me aloud. Their whispers still oozed around me like slime but it was easier for me to push those into the recesses of my mind, where they jostled for space among the silences within me. I know they still make fun of me but I am able to forget about them since they no longer loudly demand my attention.

No one but I can see the changes in my body yet. Every day I feel the gentle slope of my stomach become steeper, the just-slight fullness of my breasts, the new lustre of my hair, the glow on my skin. I am impatient for my child to announce his presence from within my body, to proclaim his impending arrival to everyone so that they know that I, Nadee, the mad woman, will be a mother. Yet a part of me wants to keep him nestled in secrecy, to keep him tucked away, to keep him… just mine. For now, both of us are invisible.

I pray for the health of my child as fears for his well-being crowd my waking thoughts and invade my sleep. I speak to his father about the baby but he is unresponsive on this matter as we seek the warmth and comfort of each other's bodies and souls, greedily grasping. Then darkness slinks away towards light and he is gone. I am left alone again. Despite my own foreknowledge, despite what I know of my child and his future I need some reassurance, something… someone to give me hope. There is only one person in Fatehpur-Sikri who can comfort me; the man who was the reason for the city's existence.

Sheikh Chishti's body has been re-interred into the new mausoleum which is crowded during the day when devotees from the village and the fort visit, praying for their desires to come true, asking the saint to intervene on their behalf. At night the marble glows in the moonlight, pearlescent and ethereal, as if with one blink of my eyes it will evaporate like a mirage. The inset gems catch the glow of the moon and shimmer in muted flower-tones of blue, green and red. There are few faithful at this time of night. A single light trapped inside a hanging lamp casts filigreed shadows on the walls. They dance as the lamp sways in the slight breeze that also ruffles my hair and cools my brow.

I sit in the corner behind one of the marble screens that looks like an insubstantial sheet of fragile lace. Within each twist of the geometrically-stylized, carved flowers flutter black strings that have been tied by the thousands of female devotees who make the pilgrimage to the Sheikh's tomb. These little pieces of string embody the hopes and trust of the scores of women who have stood behind the screen and gazed upon the shrouded marble tomb of the saint, their lips moving in silent prayer, their eyes closed as they visualize and then whisper their wants and desires.

Barren women gather years of dashed hopes into the humble cotton strings, and pray for the miracle of a child, a son. Wives tie into the strings their own fragmented and sublimated desires, asking for the long lives of their husbands and for good health for their children. Destitute widows imbue the frail thread with the hopes that were drowned within their lost destinies, begging God and the saint for a reason to go on for another day. If their prayers are answered each devotee will return with a gift for the saint's tomb, each according to what she can afford. Then carefully and gently they will untie a string, freeing the space for another's dreams and desperations.

Some of the richer ones will sponsor a night of qawwali, the Sufi ritual of songs that soar into the sky till dawn. In these songs God is the beloved and the devotee the impassioned lover, intoxicated with the purity and oneness of desire and union. But tonight all is silent as I sit within the jewelled mausoleum of Sheikh Salim Chishti.

I have no string with me, so I break off a long strand of my own hair and holding it between my fingers, pray upon it for the health of my unborn child, blowing my fervent hopes onto it. I breathe into it all I want for him, for us. Then I tie it onto the screen and I pray late into the night, long after the lingering devotees have departed. I watch my hair flutter on a marble vine that loops around on itself and know that my prayers will bear fruition. I feel this knowledge within me and feel comforted.

I wonder what my child will look like, the real possibility of a human being, not the insubstantial phantom children of my past whom I had drawn into shifting sand. My son comes into focus behind my closed eyelids. He has the round face of his father, his stocky build and dark complexion. He has my somewhat flat nose and my wavy-curly hair, though the colour is the dark-black of his father's hair. He is the perfect blend of the two of us. He is beautiful, perfect and healthy. A son of whom his father and I will be proud. He slumbers quietly within me, as if he needs his rest before he blazes into the world, setting it aflame with the brilliance of his existence.

The urge to gaze upon his face more fully overpowers me, so I slip past the guards and head to the lake, hoping a walk will calm my thoughts. The night has grown darker; the moon is resting behind a cloud, its light eerily diffused, glowing bluish-grey. I can see the radiating light from the dying fires of the weary travellers who are staying at the inn tonight. Occasionally I hear the braying of a donkey or muffled sounds of talking coming from behind the stone walls of that building.

~

The earth is hard, its surface digging into my bare feet, the rough vegetation scratching indentations into my soles. The lake shines like a mirror in the starlit night. It looks deeper tonight somehow, deeper and more mysterious as if it shelters a secret it is loath to give up. I tell the lake of my child and feel her satisfaction and happiness for me, as her gentle waves caress my feet, soothing away the scratches and aches.

The ground around the lake is more malleable, watered into softness and the perfect spot for drawing a picture of my child. Using a thin stick I draw his face over and again into the ground but his reality continues to escape me. His face that I etch into the soil is an outline, a set of too-smooth lines and curves without mobility or life. I cannot decide if the canvas is imperfect or if my vision and talent are wanting.

The lakeside is strewn with tiny sharp stones, their edges honed to perfection. I use one of these to create a living portrait on my living flesh. As the skin of my upper thigh flexes and moves, as the red liquid outlines flow, my child's face comes alive. From certain angles as I contract my muscles and shift, he smiles at me, his eyes fixed onto mine. I smile back as I caress his brow, 'My child,' I whisper and he laughs, his toothless grin radiating the pure joy of life, moving me to a moment of happiness. My blood drips past my flesh, seeping into the dry earth and I am so enraptured in joy that I do not feel the pain. Together we laugh softly in the night until the moon emerges from its cloud-rest and the darkness lightens slightly. The last fires from the courtyard of the inn succumb to the gathering night-wind, inking out the night, and then, together, we fall asleep on the ground. The almost inaudible waves of the lake sound in my ears like a lullaby.

Before I fall asleep I stare straight up at the seven bright stars that are suspended above me. I open my hand and try to grab them out of the sky, they seem so near. They are the saptarishi, the seven sages, whose penance and meditations had transformed them into brilliant stars forever looking upon the earth from the heavens. I wonder if their reflection can be seen in the high mountain lake of ice from which Yamuna emerges to flow through the mountains and then onto the plains. Thoughts of Yamuna comfort me in some strange way and I pretend I can hear her tell me a secret as I descend into sleep undisturbed by anything that happens around me.

I was only dimly aware of a shadow that flitted past me, a silhouette of black in the night, an insubstantial wraith. It was not I who sobbed that night, it was not I who wept with a pain that comes from a bottomless spring deep within, wrenched from a place where fears congeal and hopes die. It was not I who breathed rapidly and then struggled violently before stopping abruptly. I slept peacefully, unaware, unknowing, untouched. I only learned about what happened later… much later.

~

Her body floated upon the lake, bloated and saturated. No one knows how long she was part of the waters. She was discovered only when her body filled with air and bobbed up to the surface like a dead fish. One of the travellers from the emperor's inn found her, face-up, decaying eyes fixed upon the morning sky as if in wonder. First he was startled, thinking he had come upon a lone woman taking a bath in the lake. Then he noticed her puffed face, grey colour and bloated stomach and ran screaming for help.

As the men pulled her from the waters, her skin and flesh came away in their hands in silky skeins. They laid her at the edge of the lake and her husband, a small-time farmer sobbed as he looked into her ruined face and the body that streamed rivulets of water, wetting the ground on which she lay.

~

Rumours about the life of the thief and her husband spread even as he mourned his loss. They had lived in a village close to Fatehpur-Sikri. He used to coax the earth to give up its bounty in an inhospitable and rocky land. They had lived a happy life, except for the empty space within and between each of them that could only be filled by a child. They wanted a strong son to help his father on his farm, a child to fill his mother's aching arms, a support for their old age, someone to bring the joy of a new generation into their lives. The mother had not been a healthy woman, unable to withstand the heat of the sun, her eyes burning like coals embedded into her skull if she spent too much time outside. But he had loved her, they had been together since they were children. Husband and wife, partners for seven lifetimes, sharing sorrows and joys and everything that makes life what it is. Until a few nights ago, while he slept, with a smile on his lips, she had crept away.

The townsfolk and the servants who had gathered around talked with wonder as he wept, unmindful of his manliness, his dignity drowning within his sorrow at the death of his family. He showed his blistered feet to the people assembled. He had walked for miles searching for his wife, his voice growing hoarse as he called her name over and over and over again. They could see his reddened eyes that seemed to ask them all a question: why had she done this? No one could tell him the answer. They did not know.

Then he collapsed upon her covered body sobbing and incoherent. It was only then that he discovered their unformed child that lay between the dead woman's legs still attached to her body through a thick, red and grey cord, covered by her wide skirts that someone had arranged for posthumous modesty. Tenderly, the father picked up the little boy who fit snugly in his palm, his nebulous, blurred face upturned as the tears rained onto his tiny shrouded eyes.

Maybe his son had been born too early, expelled from his wife's body in a slush of blood and tissue. Sensing perhaps that there was no other recourse she had headed to the lake. She had died even as her dead child hung out of her body. She and her own child of dreams died together on that night, drowning in the water while I lay asleep by the shore. The people gathered by the lake tried to comfort the bereaved man. They failed and faltered into silence. Her story would never be told fully, her husband would never know the answers to the questions that would haunt him till he dies. This is what the dead woman's sobs tell me later that night. Her cries are trapped in the mute waters of the lake, within each grain of soil around the shores. They whisper to me of caution and tamped down hopes. She is at peace now forever, she and her child together for all eternity. But her spirit weeps for her husband and the life they would have lived together with their strong farmer son. That morning as she lay on the ground with her infant beside her, no one knew the real reasons. All they had was conjecture and half-formed macabre theories.

A whisper started there by the lake as the villagers and some guards from the fort gazed upon the dead body. This whisper blazed like a quick fire making its way into the fort, passing by the ears of Andaliib and her servants, telling me something I already knew. Soon the news made its way to the zenana and finally to the emperor's ears.

The dead woman's skin was white, like marble married to alabaster and it gleamed in the weak light of morning like bleached bone in the desert. Inside the tiny velvet purse that was still tucked into her waistband was the emperor's lost boyhood treasure.

15

Mother and Child

The wailing howl pierces the ears like the wind that used to blow into Zameerpur from the desert, pregnant with the fierce intensity of dry fire and of the power to destroy lives. It is a sound that plunges beyond pain, beyond imagination and plummets below the uncomfortable depths of misery that polite company dare not acknowledge.

The sound dissolves me from the inside out, eating away at me like acid, searing through my air ways as it burns its way out, heading determinedly towards my open mouth. From there it spills out, vibrating the air, filling it with unfathomable emotions. I try to clamp my lips together but the strength of the wails tears them open and I cannot stop… it… this thing that is happening to me. It horrifies me to realize that this howling wail is coming from within me. I close my mouth, trying to breathe in a different rhythm, trying to contain the frightening sound, but still it continues to come from a place somewhere buried deep.

The sound is equal parts horror, sadness and guilt mixed with a tinge of shame. Did the Sheikh and God spare my child and take hers in return because I prayed harder than her? Because I had more frequent access to his tomb, living inside the protected walls of the fort? Because he and I shared the same strange burden of foreknowledge? That albino woman with skin that burned and blistered in the sun, her pink eyes forever squinting into life – was her death and that of her son on my conscience forever? And was I… was I glad? Glad that it was her and not me that floated up to the top of the lake like a giant impurity? That it was her half-formed infant and not mine that lies joined to her in death through the cord of life that had made them one? That my son still lives, swimming inside me, warm and protected?

Still I mourn her. I cry for her child and the life they could have lived together with her husband. I mourn for her past and the multiple possible futures that might have been hers

~

She had been an ordinary woman, until her death which made her famous forever in the kingdom. Her death and, of course the perfect pearl that was found on her body. Sifting through rumours and swirling conversation and applying what I discover for myself through her words that float like moisture in the air, I try to re-create her life, to imagine her as she must have been once. I owe her at least this much, she tells me.

She married young and was the perfect farmer's wife. She knew how to make meals out of practically nothing, to soothe her husband's fears about the truant or too abundant monsoons; to save enough in times of bounty to tide them through the times of want. Where others saw her pale skin as strange, like the ugly underbelly of a dead fish, her husband saw in it an ethereal, moonlight-silver beauty. Through the fragile outer layer of her skin he would trace with gentle fingers the thin, blue veins of her pulsing life-blood. Under the comforting blanket of night he would watch her skin gleam in the tranquil beams of the moon. That is what he called her, Chanda – the moon.

Both of them had already forgotten the name with which she had entered his life. He never tired of gazing at his own reflection when he looked into her large eyes, fringed with colourless eyelashes. He never seemed to notice their strange pink colour. To him, she was unique, different from all other women around him, his perfect mate, the wife made for him. She was his just as he was hers.

However, even the moon has imperfections, scars and nicks and blots, and so did their marriage. The absence of a child weighed heavily on them both. Her arms felt even emptier when cascades of whispers descended around her from the other women in the village as she drew water from the well or swept the dust away from her threshold. They were hurtful, ugly whispers that overlooked her freakish appearance in favour of the even more heinous crime of being childless.

By the tenth year of her marriage she had miscarried six times and her already frail body was worn down. For her seventh pregnancy she and her husband had vowed to present the saint's tomb with a green silk sheet embroidered with the ninety-nine names of Allah. The sheet would be draped on the saint's ornate resting place, heavy with the gold thread and the fervent thanks of the parents-to-be. They asked only that the saint intercede, plead with God on their behalf and bless them as he had once blessed the emperor, with the gift of a healthy son. They sensed that this was their last chance, that her womb could no longer gather up the strength to grow another life. They poured into this pregnancy every drop of hope they could wring out of their souls.

In the second month of her pregnancy, the emperor and his army passed close to their village. Despite the toll sunlight always took on her, Chanda was determined to see the emperor, perhaps get his blessing for her unborn child. He was the representative of God on earth, ruling with the power of his divine right.

Swaddled within her sari so that no part of her skin was exposed, she sat patiently on her haunches by the roadside as the cavalcade of elephants walked by with ponderous steps. She was captivated by the pageantry, the sounds, the armour that glinted in the sun even though the glare made her avert her eyes in pain. She drank in the excitement and joy of victory that lined the weary faces of the men.

And then she saw Emperor Akbar. He was riding on a white horse which had upright ears and a long broom-like tail. A slight smile played on the emperor's sun-swarthy face as he acknowledged his people and surveyed his realm. Just then, a child from the crowd broke away from his mother and ran into the path of the procession, right in front of the emperor's horse. In a split second the horse reared and a soldier grabbed the child. After the child had been returned to the safety of his hysterical mother the emperor and his men rode away.

Chanda watched their backs recede into the distance in a giant cloud of dust, as they made their way to the fort. She felt a certain excitement burst within her, stretching its tentacles into all parts of her consciousness. She could not wait to tell her husband about this wondrous event when he returned from the fields that evening. She, a lowly, humble, farmer's wife had seen the emperor, had been in his presence and she could have sworn that he had seen her, if only for a moment.

Within that instant of drama as his horse reared up Chanda had felt as if the emperor had looked straight at her. There had been just a moment of eye contact but she felt as if her child had been blessed by her emperor. She stepped onto the road to begin the walk home, secure in the knowledge that her child was safe. He was more than safe. He was blessed by the emperor.

At first she thought she had stepped on a pebble, which dug into the sole of her bare foot. As she bent down to remove it, she saw the white-pink, round pearl glowing gently in the dust, and was entranced. She had never seen anything so beautiful in her life, so unique. Was it a sign? A gift from the emperor? Surely this rare and precious gem could only belong to him. Perhaps it was a tangible symbol of his blessing? It could not be a coincidence that out of the thousands of people lining the path he had made eye contact with her. And then she had found something that she was sure he had dropped. Dropped for her to find?

Her child stirred and kicked within her with vigour, confirming for her this connection, the meaning of this event. She closed her eyes, her shoulders slumped with relief. She could not bear to share this secret with her husband for fear that he would make her return the pearl immediately. They were poor people but honest. They would not keep what was not theirs. She did mean to return it eventually; she truly did, after the birth of her son, when all was well.

For now, however, it was her talisman. A secret joy would suffuse her as she looked at it. She kept it within a velvet purse that she had received in her dowry. The purse had been empty all these years for she had had nothing fine enough to put in it. Until now.

She tucked the purse and its precious contents into her waistband and would peek at it occasionally during the day, letting the soft glow of the gem transport her to places of escape and imagination, linking her and her child to the emperor and his blessings. Sheikh Chishti was dead. He remained only as an obscure, non-human presence under mounds of flowers and silken sheets, separated from her by lacy marble. But the emperor was flesh and blood, a divine and legendary ruler and he had looked at her, straight at her. And he had left her a symbol of his blessing. After the birth of her child she would take him and the pearl to the emperor and all would be well. He was a wise man, a good ruler and he would understand. All would be well. Until then, each day she rubbed the tiny globe that glowed from within with the protective nest of her rough peasant fingers, dreaming about her life with her child.

Then, one day, months later, she felt her child go still within her. She talked to him as she did everyday, hoping to feel his head butt her ribs, his feet kick out towards the walls of her stomach, something, anything to let her know he heard her. She was scared. This had been her longest pregnancy; the others had been expelled from her body as indistinguishable clots of blood and tissue in the first two months. But this… this child was already too-real, he communicated with her, he was blessed. He had a name, Shashi, another word for the moon. She and her husband had chosen that name one night as they talked late, staring at the moon and at the reflection of its beams bouncing off her skin.

Perhaps the baby was merely tired. Or… or he was being naughty. Children are naughty. Yes, that's what it was. He was preparing himself to be the capricious child he was meant to be. He was playing hide and seek with her. She smiled indulgently, reassuring herself for a day and then for another.

Then a new unwelcome thought slithered through her mind unbidden, though she tried her best to ignore it. It would not go away, forcing her to acknowledge it. Perhaps – a cold wind blew onto the back of her neck – her child was cursed. He was cursed by the emperor because she, his mother, was a thief. She had taken what was not hers and now she, her husband and baby were cursed by the most powerful man in the world. He had waited too long to get his treasure back, he had given her time, but now the emperor had cursed her and her child.

Word of the emperor's lost pearl had made its way to her village, his grief at the loss of his father's gift was fodder for gossip. Surely he must have cursed a million times the person who had deprived him of the one jewel he valued more than any other he possessed… and in doing so cursed the life of her innocent child.

One night as usual she smiled at her husband as she served him his dinner. And when, later, the walls of her womb became inhospitable to her silent infant and began to push him out, she knew what she had to do. There was still time. If she managed to return the jewel to the emperor perhaps the curse would be lifted and she would give birth, when she was meant to, to a healthy son.

Her husband, tired and beaten down by the highly desiccative heat of summer, was worried about his crops even when he slept. His dreams were troubled, his sleep fractured. She could not add to his burden. The impending birth of his child was the only source of happiness for him and she could not, would not deprive him of that. She never wanted him to know how close they had come to losing all their dreams. She had been the one to draw this curse upon their futures. She would find a way to reclaim their hopes and their lives. Tenderly she touched her husband's hand, before walking out into the cooling night.

~

She walks in the dark, her feet streaming blood into the ground as her hard, calloused soles are pierced by the pointed stones and rough grasses that line the way to her destination. As she approaches the lake, it shines cold like unyielding metal in the moonlight, and still, as still as the child that was beginning to push his way into the world, already dead.

She cries now, in pain and fear and despair with the knowledge that was hers and hers alone, reeling under the terrible burden of her guilt. She can see the walls of the fort loom above her. Somewhere among all those blazing lights is the emperor. She will return to him the treasure he seeks and he will release her from his curse. 'Yes, all will be well,' she says as she caresses the pulsating mound of her belly. She repeats this to herself over and over again.

She can walk no further. Agony slices through her in ribbons until she feels like she is being ripped apart. There is no one here to help, no one who can, and she spares not a glance for my sleeping form by the side of the lake.

I am smiling in my dreams, caught up in the promise of my own child. She does not see me, trapped as she is within her world of pain.

She is breathing hard and fast, panic and instinct colliding, as her labour makes her double up and stumble and then slip, falling into the lake. She cannot swim and even as she thrashes her arms about, clawing for survival, her baby slips between her legs and dangles head-down, all her fluids gushing into the lake. She tries to scream and swallows the cold water which flows into her open mouth and distended nostrils. It burns like fire on the way down for one prolonged, agonizing instant before it gushes into her lungs, drowning her. Her body twitches and then relinquishes the last vestiges of life. Then she feels nothing any more. Together mother and child sink into the waveless depths of Fatehpur Lake.

~

By the time I reach the lakeside, someone has thrown a sheet over the bodies as they prepare to lift Chanda and her baby for the final phase of their earthly journey. Her husband is staring at the covered mound, silent, his tears flowing unchecked.

One of her arms has escaped the folds of the sheet and it is blindingly white, fragile-looking and defenceless against the sun's fury as it beats down upon her. Silently he leans over and tucks it back inside the sheet. His hand lingers on her skin, stroking it gently once before retreating to his side.

Growing past his shock is a tiny kernel of grief that will explode into life in the coming months. He will never know for certain the relationship between his wife and the pearl. He will never truly know what happened during the time between the moment when his wife smiled sweetly at him at dinner time and when he awoke to find her gone. This lack of knowing will soon melt into his anguish and form a single question. And that is the question he will repeat over and over again even on his own deathbed. His second wife and two sons will then take on the heavy mantle of that mysterious question but they will not be able to decode it and will have no ability to answer him when he asks; 'Where did you get it Chanda?' They will wonder about his dying query till the end of their own lives and pass it down as family lore through their generations.

This afternoon, however, he is still wrapped inside the muffling quilt of grief and shock, unaware and uncaring about the rest of his life. So I look at him with pity and understanding and stand beside him silently as he helps lift his family for the last time and departs with her and his child to relinquish them to the purifying fire. He does not even notice I am there. I am glad.

~

Under cover of night I press his palm over my rapidly beating heart; right on the spot that marks his place in my life and wait for my panic to subside. I trace the scar of his remembrance and then I place my own palm over the back of his hand and press hard until it feels as if he holds my heart within an embrace of comfort. It calms me, and I feel the restless racing rhythm slow down, gradually, finally.

'I cannot lose him. He is mine, my child, my son. I cannot bear to lose him as once I lost you,' I whisper. I feel him move behind me, curving his arm to hug me close. He comes to me as he does almost every night, in silence, cloaked in darkness, suffused with mystery.

This child will be all I have, my shield and protection, my greatest accomplishment. The knowledge of Chanda's fate streaks like a comet of fear inside me, blazing across my thoughts, paralysing me.

Tonight I am ravenous, my hunger is unsubsiding, relentless and bottomless and I turn towards him.

'Each night I die a thousand deaths in your arms,' I whisper, 'I feel you, but you never speak. Why don't you ever speak to me any more?'

In the quiet I can sense his smile as his lips move down my body and I try to decipher his silent messages meant only for me. In the gathering silence my skin is heightened with pinpricks of awareness and suddenly I want to be away from this place. With just him and I and our child. To escape my destiny and slough off all the burdens I carry. My voice weaves a spell around both of us as I speak to him softly.

'Make me forget. Make me forget her and this place. Make me forget everything, I want to not think about anything. Just for tonight.'

He does.

16

No Questions

Some bruises do not start out blue and purple. They do not fade into yellow and disappear into nothingness. They are invisible; these bruises that wrap themselves around me like a skin absorbing all of my body into themselves.

The border of each bruise melts into the next, bleeding their colour into each other, shaded and indistinct like my memories. Memories of my childhood that drift back to me like solitary, drifting leaves borne on a gentle wind, forcing me to retrace my life up to this point. I see the scenes in my mind, like a shadow-play on rough, earthen walls.

~

Brown furrows, like the tracks of a giant serpent, tear the earth open. I run behind my father as he ploughs our fields, opening up rich, loamy seams in which he will plant seeds and water them to life and maturity, protecting them against marauding birds and thieving cattle and men. I can see only his back, bare and burned nut-brown, wet with sweat. I am trying, I am trying even now to see his face but I cannot. I am laughing with the joy of running and then I am stopped abruptly. I cannot move my feet as much as I try. 'Baba... Baba,' I shout, asking him to turn towards me, so I can catch a glimpse of his face. But he keeps on his path, walking resolutely, his back dripping sweat, his steps weary. Mud oozes around my feet, trapping me while he keeps walking away... away... away.

The night breeze is cold, chilling me to the bone. In our courtyard, my mother has made a fire and the three of us sit around it, warming our hands, watching the dancing flames which are creating fantastic creatures and strange and wonderful stories. The flames twist and writhe like fluid serpents and I am lost, fascinated by their red-gold dance. I feel my mother's hand stir the air around my head, a whisper of a sound, as if she is getting ready to caress my hair. All my life, she has striven not to become too attached to me, not to express her love too much. A daughter is someone else's treasure after all. She will leave to live in another's house. Too much affection will only make the pain of loss keener for me and for her. This night, safe in my home, I smile, anticipating her touch, but then I feel nothing. I look back, up in the direction of her face, and see nothing but dark, empty night. Where is she?

I have forgotten my father's face. And my mother's. He is just a tired, bare back. She is but a voice. Sometimes an angry, shrill voice that reprimands me; sometimes a dreamy, gentle one as she speaks to me under cover of night, stripped down to her vulnerabilities, as she tells me stories and prepares me for my life. Both are trapped in my past, within the tendrils of the water hyacinth which tries to drag me into its lair of treacherous memories each night.

So far I have travelled. From the river of secrets to the river of stories to this dusty, craggy place. From the King of the Dead to the King of the World. From madwoman to soothsayer.

Yes, they no longer call me mad. For I can predict events, forecast things that have not yet happened. That is what they say. I know who... what I am. I live under my own foreknowledge which tightens its coils around me until I feel squeezed and constricted and ready to give up. Give up? And do what? I do not know.

How was I able to foretell the return of the emperor's treasure, they ask. How did I know of the woman with pale skin? How did I know about her velvet purse? I do not know how to answer them. My foreknowledge tells me only of events that are of importance to me, that will affect the trajectory of my own life along its predestined path. I cannot foretell the final reckonings of the emperor's many wars. But I fear if I speak these thoughts aloud, they will brand me with other names, more dangerous ones, like traitor and heretic and rebel.

I dare to make the emperor incidental, an afterthought in the journey of my own life, when his status is to rule over everything and everyone? This is arrogant blasphemy, even for a soothsayer. I remain silent.

Even if I never foretell another event again, my life will be made comfortable forever. The looks of derision and scorn have turned to avarice and resentment. How dare I, strange madwoman, bring this simple, yet all important joy to the emperor's life? How dare I become important? Not invisible any more? The emperor asked me what I wanted. He wanted to give me a reward for my efforts, for my vision.

'We shall give you anything you want. Ask,' he commanded as I stood before him.

His fingers restlessly caressed the pearl which he held in the palm of one hand, the velvet purse carelessly discarded, inside out, its lining exposed, on the ground in front of him.

I follow the movement of his fingers as they glide over the tiny white-pink globe and I wonder if he can sense the heat and the trapped longing of the woman who had possessed it for those two months. Do Chanda's fears and hopes and desires seep through the dense core of the pearl and transmit themselves to his soul? Or can he only feel his father's presence on that long-ago night when the gem came into his possession? Can his fingers sense the palpable change in his childhood treasure? Does he know it is changed forever?

Does he wonder about Chanda? About that poor, drowned woman and her baby? Does he even know her name? Does he realize his connection to her? Does he remember her standing patiently on the side of the road? Or was she just one of the crowd, another faceless citizen of his realm?

'I want two things above all,' I say. His fingers slow their movement and I hear the waters from the fountains gurgle in anticipation. Again, we are in the zenana, among his wives and children and concubines, seated upon the stone platform in the middle of the artificial pond. The world awaits my answer so I speak.

'I want a house of my own. Not here, but outside… just outside the walls of the fort so I can visit the saint's tomb… or do anything else as and when I wish. A small house, all my own. It should have a courtyard in the centre of which should grow a young, pomegranate tree.' My voice stills as I swallow convulsively. I continue.

'I am with child… and… and I want no questions from anyone… ever.' I let the heavy, rough cotton shawl I wear slip down to the floor and feel every eye focus upon my now swollen belly. My hands instinctively encircle my girth protecting my son from those pointed gazes.

A few smothered gasps, a few mutterings about my shamelessness and some quickly recited prayers were all that followed. No one would ever ask me about my child's father or when he was conceived. To do so would be to gain the emperor's wrath.

Before I turn to leave, I raise my eyes to his, for an instant, 'She didn't steal it you know. She thought you gave it to her. She was going to return it after the birth of her child. She thought it was a blessing… from you.' Did I imagine that his face turned contemplative as I turned to leave? Did a flicker of remembrance burn into brief light inside his eyes? Did he feel compassion for her? Sadness?

~

My presence cleaves through the fort like my father's plough had torn open the ground. I walk into and leave behind waves of silence. A silence that is loaded with curiosity, venom, jealousy and wonder. Andaliib's servants scatter before me as I return to my room to gather up my meagre belongings and leave for my new home. They dare not speak to me now; they dare not make fun of me.

Andaliib is at home, downstairs, drinking tea like she always does in the middle of the afternoon. I can smell the clove and cardamom which infuses her favourite, coppery beverage as I walk towards her sitting room. It is hot and one of her servants is standing behind her with a large, ornately decorated reed fan. It cuts through the heat with a swishing sound, circulating cool air around her. I notice that escaped tendrils of her hair dance in this artificial breeze. Her eyes are closed, her eyelids and forehead glistening with sweat.

'I am leaving,' I say to her.

'So I hear… soothsayer,' she responds, looking past me at the wall. I do not know what I had expected. A declaration of my importance in her life? Gratitude for saving her life, for staying with her through all the changes in her status? An acknowledgment of some kind? Something… anything. I turn to leave.

'You tried to warn me,' I see her swallow the lump in her throat as she forces the words out, 'that night.'

'Yes,' I say, 'but it was predestined so I could not stop it and neither could you. It… those events, brought you here. And this is your place in life. This is where you belong.'

She lies back on the scattered pillows and closes her eyes again, arching her neck to catch more of the breeze from the fan. Her voice is little over a whisper but I hear it anyway: 'I hope you too find the place that is meant to be yours in life… Nadee.'

~

My house is small and built out of the large, grey stones that are cut out of the cliffs in the area. It stands just outside the walls of the fort-city of Fatehpur-Sikri. As a soothsayer, sometime courtier, I need to be close enough to answer the emperor's summons, so each night I go to bed with the shadow of his fortress darkening the inner courtyard where I sleep during these hot summer nights. This little house is almost exactly like my home in Zameerpur. The courtyard, the orientation, the rooms and their sizes, I have recreated a part of my past, a legacy for my child. Everything here reminds me of my first home, except for the pomegranate tree that stands to one side of the courtyard.

The tree has surrendered to the heat of summer and shed all its leaves. I water it every day knowing that when the heat fades away I will be rewarded by its new leaves, its incomparable pink blossoms, their heady perfume and finally its fruit. Fruit that when cut will bleed garnet fluid like a fresh, gushing wound and will taste as sweet as the love I feel for my child and for his father. This is my home, this little house just outside the walls of the fort, close enough for my nightly visits to the Sheikh's tomb where I pray for the health of my son. I am content. It is a rather curious feeling but one that I know will be fleeting so I try and savour it, elongating the time, drawing out the pleasure and getting to know a calm joy.

Sometimes after visiting the Sheikh's mausoleum, I make my way to the paanch mahal, the palace of five levels. I climb up each successively smaller storey until I reach the domed cupola which is bordered by filigreed red sandstone balconies. The flames of the flickering torches and the light cast by the many oil lamps bounce off the red walls bathing everything in a pink-gold hue.

I lean against the low balcony and look beyond the walls of the fort into the shaded darkness that lies beyond. During the day, the eye can see a patchwork of fields and orchards, houses and the trees and craggy hills of the environs. At night all I can see are indistinct shapes that become more defined yet somehow even more ghostly, seeming to drift closer the harder I stare at them.

~

'I do not dream any more,' the woman says. I have seen her before, on previous visits to the zenana. Always on the fringes, looking on, listening, as if trapping everything she saw and heard into her voracious memory. Her skin sags around her bones, a tent over a finely constructed, royal skeleton. She is the emperor's aunt, sister of his father; a princess who has lived many lives, who has endured many lifetimes in transition.

Princess Gulbadan was born in Kabul and her arrival into the world had heralded her father Babar's ascent to his ruthlessly-won throne of Hindustan. She has been a princess, a refugee, a prisoner of war… a wife, a widow, even a mother of a child, a son she never talks about – whom no one talks about.

I force myself to listen to her, impatient for my nightly visitor. Tonight I am nervous, my mind skittering from one thought to the next and I cannot concentrate on her. Her voice is ragged, like a wisp of mist, yet its insistent tone brings me back to her presence. 'Did you hear me soothsayer? I dream no more.'

'Perhaps you need a rest from dreams?' I ask. I wish I could have a few nights without dreams. A few nights from which I could awaken refreshed and alive, without this vague sense of disquiet that follows me like a faithful dog.

She is silent for a moment then she says, 'Without dreams I am nothing.'

I do not know how to answer her. Instead I ask, 'What do you mean?' I know the answer but she needs the question to be asked. She needs to formulate the answer and say the words out aloud.

She has been waiting a long time for someone to ask her this question. 'I write down whatever there is that I have heard and remember,' she tells me as if reciting the original royal command that has made her, Princess Gulbadan, a chronicler of her age and times. She peers from behind the protected walls of the zenana, writing down everything she observes, and everything she experiences. She talks to the maids, the female guards and the eunuchs to glean information about the world outside, of the court and the emperor who rules over everything. She is hungry for any news. When she sleeps she transforms what she learns into delicate prose in her dreams. In her dreams, she says, she sits in the gardens of the Kabul she remembers from her childhood. Shaded from the sun by a tree, she writes history with a quill made of a peacock feather. The words flow from her mind and through the ink, like rivers of knowledge. Now she is, however, at an impasse for her dreams have evaporated.

'I remember the past only in dreams,' she says. 'If I try to recall actual events I fear I will sink into a grief so deep that I will never surface. So I dream and then awaken and write it all down on paper. The taste of apricots in Kabul, sweet and golden… like sunlight mingling with crisp mountain breezes. I remember the face of my father, that fierce, sunburned warrior's face, as he smiled at me, when I was a child of eight. He embraced me once you know? Yes, he did when he came to visit my lady Mahan… my Senior Mother. That is all I remember of him, an embrace and a smile. After all those years on the run, those moments of intense fear and snatched-away joys, his face and his embrace are all I remember of my father. I have to… I have to dream as I have done for years, or else how will I follow the command of my emperor? Tell me soothsayer, when will my dreams return?'

'That depends on you,' I tell her, 'what are you willing to give up in return for your dreams?'

'Anything. Everything. They are all I have left.'

'Can you give up writing them down yourself? Can you give up control?' I ask softly.

'But… but it is a royal decree, a command from my emperor. He has asked of me only this one thing in all my life. A petty thing in exchange for all he has lavished on me. How can I not obey?' She falls silent.

'He will never know,' I tell her, impatient to leave, 'you will still record your history as His Majesty wishes. You will just not write it yourself. You cannot write down your dreams. For in doing so you dilute their power and without that they are nothing. Perhaps… perhaps you can tell me your dreams instead and I can write them down for you. I will be your hand, that grips the quill and does the bidding of the words that come out of your mouth.' Reluctantly, she gives in. Finally, I am able to leave and make my way home.

~

You are not a dream my love, and neither is our child. Dreams are echoes of the past; they are cold fingers of dread, whereas we live in a future of sweetly endless possibilities. As I trace my fingers through the grooves and dips of your face and feel your beard rasp against my skin I come alive. And when I talk to our son and touch him through the thin barrier of my skin I grasp reality in my hands.

Reality is touchable fact. Dreams are useless flotsam. You smile against my cheek in the dark and together we lie on our sides, feeling the energetic kicks that pulsate my skin outwards, and I know our child is alive. Perhaps tonight I shall not dream.

17

Torrent of Dreams

The waters of Fatehpur Lake have changed. I sense this change one hot afternoon as I sit by its shores. My feet are submerged within the cool depths of the lake as I am trying to escape the dry heat that shimmers around me. I feel a strange difference slip in through my pores, enveloping me from the inside, before travelling to my brain, sparking my thoughts. The water caresses me still, slathering its liquid over my skin, sending a cool surging through my veins, washing away the sweat from my pores. I realize that the lake is no longer a mere mute receptacle for my stories, an innocent, circumscribed body of water. Its gentle waves are being bathed in something they cannot fully understand, for they are but a vehicle, a means. For the first time it has recognized a power within itself and it is seduced by the newness of it all.

The sun slowly lists across the sky, as if dragged unwilling, red streaks begin to appear, bleeding across the horizon. From the waters, now reflected crimson like a pool of watery blood, I hear a laughing whisper from a voice I had heard only in a dream, 'Look how the sky bleeds. So shall his realm.'

Fatehpur Lake is no longer without a voice. It has an identity. As Chanda had taken her last breath, inhaling water from the lake deep into her lungs, she had given to it her voice, which was imbued with her spirit, her feelings and her desires, in exchange. And then as she had lain beneath the surface she and the lake had merged, washing their stories into each other. Now they are indistinguishable. They are one. I can hear her fury and her anguish, the words seething like a poison she cannot wait to release into the world.

She is furious at losing her love, her life, her son and she blames one person and one place for all these losses: Emperor Mohammad Jalal-ud-Din Akbar, the Refuge of the World, and Fatehpur-Sikri, the site of her death. She wants to exact her revenge on them. She had tried, tried so hard to make things right, pleading and crying out for help, but to no avail. No one came to her aid; not her fate, not even me, lying fast asleep entranced in my dreams. The emperor, instead of protecting her, his loyal subject had cursed her for her minor transgression and that she could not forgive. She had died just outside the walls of this great capital city and no one had heard her, no one had helped her. They had been unconcerned by her anguish but she would be obsessed with theirs. She is determined that the emperor and his capital shall suffer unspeakably. That is the only salve her wounded, trapped soul seeks.

Now, in her newfound incarnation, she has power that the emperor can only imagine, the lake tells me. She exults in this knowledge like a petulant, excited child and I fear nothing can stop her. Her malevolence frightens me. It goes beyond even Ganga's vindictiveness, this targetted hatred. Though she lives on within Fatehpur Lake she hates even its waters for their entry into her body had caused her death. All that is left of her, bereft of her body and of her life, distilled into just her essence is hatred. And it is growing by the instant.

She does not remember love, the gentle love she had for her husband, the protective love she had borne for her child, her love for her simple life: all are forgotten in her new form. All she remembers are the emotions that had torn through her in her dying moments. Emotions that could only be satiated by destruction and desolation. She tells me of the terrible things she wishes upon the people of Fatehpur-Sikri and above all, their emperor. I try to reason with her, to dissuade her. I tell her it was her destiny, that the people of the village and the new city are innocent, that they bear no burden of guilt. She does not listen to me. That is another change; the lake has exchanged the gift of speech for deafness. I listen helplessly to her curses and to the revenge that spreads out in ripples of increasing force. She grows stronger each day, more vocal, purifying and concentrating her hatred, and I am amazed at the transformation of that once-gentle woman into this vitriolic force.

She gurgles with laughter as she tells me a secret. Even in the moment of her death she had birthed the destruction of the city. As she had stumbled through the dark to her final destination, she had picked up something quite unknowingly. Borne on the winds that blew hard the night of her death had flown a single, innocuous-looking seed. A gust had blown it into the rough weave of her sari, trapping it securely by her body. Tightly tucked inside that little kernel lay the unfurled final destinies of many, including my own.

With the omniscience of death, freed from the bonds of her body, she can now clearly observe the path and trajectory of that seed. As she and her child lay together at the bottom of the lake, the seed had swelled with water. Detaching itself from her it had fallen away, sinking into the rich, loamy clay of the lake-bed. There it had lain dormant until now. Already it is beginning to germinate and sprout, growing into a mighty plant. A water hyacinth is starting to bloom in the depths of Fatehpur Lake and it will change the destiny of this place and all of us, forever.

~

'My father loved gardens… and water. Like a wanderer in a desert, he longed to recreate the dramatic, colourful landscape of his childhood and youth in the dusty plains of Hindustan. He created a garden at Sikri you know? Much before my nephew built this city of dreams here; when it was still a small stone-cutters' village. Before the saint made this village home, my father planted a beautiful garden here. A paradise garden.' Gulbadan Begum's pride in her family, especially for her father and her nephew, shines through her words like freshly minted copper.

Her dreams have returned in a torrent, and the words gush from her lips, tumbling one over the other, until the quill clutched in my fingers breaks, splattering blobs of ink on to the paper. Still she continues, as if she does not see this, oblivious to my cramped fingers clenching and unclenching themselves. As if she does not see me massage the small of my tired back from which spasms are radiating through my body, jolting my little one out of his slumber.

I resent being the medium of her writing, though I had been the one to suggest this solution to her. The history that she has lived through seems fake to me, contrived somehow. The stories of her ancestors struggle to come alive under my pen. She relates them to me as if by rote. She recounts tales of great privation and majestic valour, of poverty and grandeur, of victories and defeats. But she seems through it all, a removed observer, moving from one place to the next depending on the whim of each successive ruler. She has had, until now, no voice and no role. She is a relic, an old woman well past death. She is an assumed responsibility and she knows this. She was selected from all the women in the zenana for this one job because she has lived through the reigns of three emperors.

She desperately wants to live up to her responsibilities, to be a person that history will not forget because she will bequeath it her words. I cannot begrudge her these needs. Still, as we sit in her quarters in the zenana, I find my resentment growing. I seek the source of this feeling.

This history that I write for her upon paper is merely stories; they do not smell of reality. Reality needs to be carved into something living; it involves pain, not effortless dreams. Reality needs to be drawn out from the depths of tears and embedded into your soul, reaching into the depths of the past to grasp at something living and imprint itself upon the present. I know my own destiny is woven into the fabric of hers and so my hand continues its journey across the rough paper.

I write her stories, my hand moving as if on its own volition and I get lost in my own dreams of my future and try to shake off the past that threatens to tie me down.

Gulbadan Begum never talks about her husband, the man who had given her a child and helped to consolidate the kingdom for her brother and her nephew. And what of her son? He is absent from these stories, his presence a void in her life.

If I had not heard the rumours and felt his presence within her, not felt her kindred-mother soul, I would have suspected she was childless. Her body had nurtured a child from conception until birth. The harem talks about her son, a living child who had somehow vanished. He had disappeared from her presence within a kingdom wreathed in mysteries and far-flung empire building, intrigue and murder. And yet, she shows no sorrow, no pain at this most paramount loss.

'Do you wonder where he is? Your son?' I ask, interrupting the flow of her words. She looks at me befuddled as my question wrenches her away from the pleasant memories of her past.

'Do you dream of him?' I ask.

'No,' she says.

I wonder which of my questions she has answered.

She dreams only of her past life as if the present and the future are unimportant, less tangible. She talks of her childhood in the court of her father, the first Mughal emperor of Hindustan, Babar. His death, when she was but a child, resonates within her nightmares. It was the death of a stranger with whom she remembers barely one tender afternoon, a hug and a kiss when she was eight. Her life had been changed forever by his passing. As an orphaned princess she had become a refugee and a commodity, useful only for building alliances.

She tells me in elegant and understated language that her heart still weeps at the fate of her beloved brother Hindal and stirs with rage and hatred against his murderer, their half-brother and her captor, Kamran. She camouflages her true feelings by muting them with flowery verse and delicate sentiments. To do less, to show her true emotions and thoughts, would be unseemly for a royal princess, the aunt of the emperor, a gentle lady from a bygone age.

Prince Kamran had offered to free her on the condition that she write to her husband, a man she rarely saw, Khizr Khwaja Khan, urging him to side with him against Humayun. She is proud still of what she said to Prince Kamran so long ago, 'Khizr Khwaja Khan has no way of recognizing a letter from me. I have never written to him myself. He writes to me when he is away, by the tongue of his sons. Write yourself what is in your mind.'

She repeats this story often; her one act of defiance perhaps, in a life spent travelling according to others' whims. She cries when she recalls the murder of her brother at the hands of Kamran. And she is angry that despite his defeat and capture, the Emperor Humayun demurred against punishing Kamran's treason with execution.

'Brotherly custom has nothing to do with ruling and reigning. If you wish to act as a brother, abandon the throne. If you wish to be king, put aside brotherly sentiment.' She repeats these words of a long-dead courtier of Emperor Humayun with passion. Sheltering her own feelings and intent within the words of another gives her both voice, as well as immunity from having her loyalty to the emperor questioned. 'He was blinded, his eyes run through with a white-hot blade,' she says, 'though his treason deserved death. It would have made my heart glad to see him killed.' I see the roiling hatred rage into a storm behind her usually sedate and dignified persona. Trying to hide her anger, she takes a deep breath before saying, 'Truly the Emperor Humayun, my brother, was merciful and kind. He did what he considered best. It is not for me, a mere woman, to question the acts of emperors.'

She spends many hours in the gardens. They remind her of her childhood in Kabul. With its lush hillsides and white-topped mountains, Kabul is a shimmering mirage into which she dreams her dreams of the past. She repeats the same stories over and over again, when she speaks of the nectar-like apricots and the grapes whose juicy sweetness could not be erased in her memory despite the passing of decades.

In this way, we are similar, she and I. We are both caught helplessly within the meshed nets of the past. Except I carry my future within myself and she has left that too behind, caught like a hapless fly, in the vaguely drawn web of her past. Somewhere along the way she has ceased being a woman and has become instead a chronicler, a mute, defenceless witness to history, mere human baggage that travels with every ruler.

She stops to take a breath and I massage my tired back. I notice that we are left alone, that as soon as I enter the gates of the zenana I carve a path through the women and children. They may cast no open aspersions; they may ask no questions aloud. But I see a million questions and condemnations in their quickly-averted eyes. I see them hurry their daughters away for fear of my contaminating presence.

To them, we are two mad women. The old aunt and the soothsayer who helps her write the chronicles of her past. I am the soothsayer who predicted the return of Gulbadan Begum's dreams and the narration of her history.

'The empress is curious about you,' Gulbadan Begum says, in one of the rare instances when she seems to return to the present. 'She is worried about her son, the crown prince, Salim. She says he is will ful and haughty and she frets. She fears,' her voice dropped lower, 'that he will one day rebel against his father. This she asked me to tell you.'

'She is right to be worried,' I tell her, 'for he will sorely test the limits of his father's patience and the boundaries of this realm. But she is powerless to change his destiny.'

A curtain flutters somewhere behind me. I sit with my back towards the inner apartments of Gulbadan Begum's house and sense someone staring at me. I know she is there, that this conversation was a carefully orchestrated event and not mere idle chatter.

I know the Empress Jodha Bai is worried, but it is beneath her to speak to me face to face. She is scared too of my reputed madness, of my mysterious pregnancy. Yet she is compelled, chastened by her mother-need to protect her son even if it is by consulting me. I continue talking though the words come out unbidden, for if I could stop them I would. They thrust me again towards naked vulnerability, towards the destiny that is inexorably mine.

'A battlefield of blood is stirring to life in the west. When the emperor departs he must never come back to this place. If he does return, you will all…' and I turn around now to stare at the silhouette behind the curtain, '…be destroyed. Your futures and your presents are cursed as long as they are tied to this place. This ruination is your immediate danger. Everything else shall pass.' This has been my home for too long. I cannot let Chanda destroy it all.

I hear a quickly-inhaled breath, a stifled sob and then footsteps rushing away. My eyes burn into those of the old woman seated in front of me and I know what she has done. I know why she does not talk about her son. I know also why she will never leave this place. I see the realization within her eyes as she knows that I know her secret.

'I am tired. This has been enough for today,' she says.

~

I do not want to leave this place, my love. This is where our son was conceived. This is where I have to stay and bring him forth from the depths of my body. This is now my home, my refuge, my power and I cannot abandon it. I am afraid above all that if I go from here, you will be lost to me, this time forever. And that I cannot bear. You will not leave me, will you? Why do you smile? See, I know you so well. I can tell that you are smiling. Why do you not answer me? Answer me.

The darkness of night is lightened by the full moon; the stars are like low-hanging luminous fruit. I can still see the red tinge that runs like a blush through the sky, prominent even in the dark. How many lives will be lost in this latest war? I know that the earth in Punjab will be washed with blood, which will soak into the ground and provide nourishment to the crops that will flourish there for years to come.

As I lie in my bed and inhale the smell of the blossoming pomegranate tree I know that the news of rebellion in Punjab has reached the emperor. His soldiers are preparing for war and they will set out for their latest campaign tomorrow. Emperor Akbar himself heads this army for it is of prime importance and he trusts no one but himself. He has consulted his astrologers who have ensured that his stars are favourably aligned. Just that morning I had told him that victory though slow and sometimes uncertain, would eventually be his.

This night as he steels himself for battle, preparing himself for a life away from the refined grandeur of his court, he kisses his pearl. As always that action relaxes him for through it he feels his mother's kisses and tears and his father's blessings. He does not know yet that he will never return to this place.

In the silence I hear Chanda laugh. The reddened night sky is reflected in shimmers on the body that is now hers and she takes it all within herself. She does not know what is about to happen but she knows something is stirring, coming to life. There is a change in the air, a charge of excitement as the realm prepares for war. Fear and exhilaration mingle with danger and she is confident that she had something to do with all of this.

She is wrong but I dare not tell her that. Her hatred burns like a furnace, so dense and yet unfocused that it is incapacitating her. It is becoming its own destruction and hers. I realize, with a dawning knowledge, that Chanda is trapped within the waters of Fatehpur Lake and she has no powers outside its perimeter. Our collective salvation lies only in letting her believe she has ultimate power.

~

A sizzling, hot, smooth blade thrusts its way inside me, so silently and quickly that for an instant I do not feel it. Then the delayed reaction of the pain hits me and I spasm into movement. My abdomen contracts in giant convulsions and my child lurches within me, preparing himself for his entry into my world.

I call aloud to my servant and she hurries to my side.

I cry out one name over and over again. I want you here, with me, grasping my hand as we welcome our child together. But you have left already… left early… and my cries do not reach you. I gather your scent close to me, within myself. I slip through the moorings of my consciousness and give birth to our child. Our son. He is here at last.

18

Retribution

I am caught. After years of deft escapes and near misses it has me. Trapped within the tightening grip of my foreknowledge, I am securely held within the grasp of the giant water hyacinth. I scream in agony as the slithery vines tighten painfully around my flesh, digging into it, raising welts, as I panic and inhale water. My chest burns as the water gurgles within me. I feel an indescribable pain merged with an agonizing sadness. I am frantic to find out yet terrified of discovery. I feel the almost unobtrusive tightening of the water about me. It is becoming thicker, more viscous, of a different texture.

Burning pain, hot licks of flame-like razors slicing neatly between thin layers of my skin, leaking into my blood, leaving no part of me untouched. Heart beating… fast… fast… fast… slow… fast… slow… slow. I will it to stop, to just stop beating, but it does not obey, for it is too far away from me now, my renegade heart. It beats in thuds of pain, refusing to stop. It beats a rhythm into the water, disturbing the ripples that radiate away from me in ever-widening swirls. It beats in time to the heart of my child. My son. Where is he?

~

Every part of me, body, mind and soul is a traitor. I am suddenly aware of my flat belly, my deflated breasts, and my un-motherlike body. I flounder as the questions struggle to be formed within my brain. I know the intent but the words are hidden under the weight of quilted mountains of pain that threaten to suffocate me, smothering my voice into silence. My voice emerges from within me, shaky and weak. I sit up in bed, my legs tucked under me, as I try to look around me.

'Where is he? Where is my son? What have you done with him?'

My hot tears fall on the portrait of my child that has healed into dark brown lines on my skin. He smiles at me and my body responds with a flood of pain. It is physical: my body hurts in anguish to hold him, suckle him, to nurture him on my dreams and stories and set him forth into the world that was meant to be his. 'Where are you? Cry out… cry loud. Your voice will guide me to you. Cry out and I will hear you. Where are you? Tell me… tell me. I will not let this separation happen. I will come to you. Cry for me. Cry…'

~

'There was no baby.' I hear the words, final and resounding, and they sound like fire crackling on wood, singeing heat leaping through them, burning through my ruined hope.

'I have seen nothing like this. Hai Allah, she is surely cursed and she will bring the curse of this mad childlessness to others among us.' This midwife's voice is old. It quavers with fear and another darker, more hateful emotion. Revulsion. Though I struggle to remain aware, I lose the battle and sink down into the lashing tentacles of unconsciousness.

They are lying, of course. My servant and the mid-wife are lying to me because they have stolen my perfect child. And they are lying even as I slip in and out of a sleep that lets me make no movement and delivers to me only snatches of conversations. They are spinning elaborate webs of lies because they have kidnapped my child.

He was… is… too perfect. Too beautiful and too good. They saw the pure radiance of his countenance and they sensed that he was special. He was destined for greatness so they have spirited him away.

This is what I had been anticipating. This is the destiny I had struggled to escape. This was the indistinct nothingness, the gaps between my foreknowledge and my reality where a horrific terror lives, breathes and grows. Even though I had known the end of this journey forever, I had allowed the joy of my child to cloud my vision. Unnoticed, my changing body and future child had chased away the one thing I should have feared, the one destiny I should have tried to escape. I was blind to my own burden.

My child is lost. No… no… I cannot accept it. The soreness of my body still holds memories of him. My heart, my mind, my soul feel as if something precious has been wrenched away with great force. How can I accept it? I know the truth after all. I know that my child is real and alive. Somewhere he waits for me.

I am outside myself for a long moment. I see my life speed up and slow down behind my closed eyelids. Then I feel screams tear out of me and drown out the world and its sensations. I exist isolated and sealed. In a terrible burst, a moment of pure clarity burns like a bright flame within my mind. And for the first time since my journey began I see for myself what I had done as I took my first steps into tentative womanhood. I know.

~

I had killed him. Caught between my grief and confusion, manipulated despite myself by Ganga and her maddening suggestions, conflicted by my own desires I had killed him: my protector, my guardian, my seduced lover. He had walked trustingly into my snare, beguiled by my desperate madness and terribly mystery. He did not want to die. I had ascribed thoughts, motivations and feelings that were not his. I was not his salvation. I was his murderer. I had killed the father of this child my arms ache to hold. How did I deserve the joy of motherhood when I had killed the man who had given my child life?

Instead of waiting with him until all life had slipped away from him, I had run away leaving him to die alone. Fled as he had grown ice-cold, stiffened in death, the blood spreading in a smoothly viscous dark pool around him. I had been afraid. I knew that I would have been punished, executed perhaps, for daring to murder

Kashi's king. My escape had been successful. No one could have found me. I had slipped away like a shadow, using my madness as my weapon and my survival. No one could have found me but him, the one I had wronged above all. And he had found me.

I had failed to account for the bewildered anger and betrayed trust of Kashi's most powerful man. I had stolen away his life, his destiny. I had forcibly twisted the skeins of his existence into the tapestry of mine and had entrapped him as surely as I myself was caught now.

I had created and recreated him within my mind until I made him real. He was real. He is real. Except now, in his long-awaited revenge, he too is gone away from me. Giving me this flash of lucid consciousness, he has left me, even as our son started to enter the world, when I needed his father the most. Without goodbyes or open recriminations, he had slipped away quietly and departed. He has left me as I had left him.

I ask him aloud whether this punishment will last for an eternity or will my broken, tasselled self be enough for him to return to me? I already know the answer to my desperately grasping questions. I know he will never return. And what of my son? Will I ever cradle him in my arms? Even if it is for just one instant I know I can imbue him with the love of a thousand lifetimes so that he will forever know the touch of his mother, her smell, her being. And I can live on through him. Within each question I ask, is nestled like a tight bud, its exact and unrelenting answer. I am compelled to ask the questions. I await no response. I know all the answers already.

My eyelids seem glued together as if I know somehow that if I open my eyes and see the empty space in my bed which my child should have occupied I will never be myself in any measure again. I give up trying to come awake and scream out the questions that are beating their thorned wings inside my head, shattering me from the inside. There is no response but silence.

~

The flowers of the water hyacinth are lilac-purple. They are beautiful, the petals large and waxen, the vines tough yet supple, the leaves like rafts, floating on the water. Springing from a single seed, the plant is now creeping its way across the lake.

It is a marauding, live presence that spreads across lakes and ponds, choking them, covering their surface and leaving nothing but an expansive, webbed tapestry of vines and leaves and flowers as it drinks thirstily, transforming water into unusable marsh. People may try to hack away at its branches and roots but once the water hyacinth has made its home in a body of water all battles are in vain. It always wins the war.

I want to wash these past years from my skin, scrub my flesh, rinse my mind and soul clean and start afresh. I want to expunge from my body the memories of my child. His loss stabs me repeatedly in a million ways until I feel like I am a giant, open wound. I want to seal in the touch of the Dom Raja. What name shall I give our relationship that transcended death and betrayal and resurrection and desertion? I have no one word with which I can call him, no one word with which to summon his memory and his presence.

I am hanging upside down, my feet caught securely within the vines. I am adrift. My hair streams below me in a saturated sheet of impermeable thick black. It moves in a flattened swathe and for a moment I am distracted despite myself and move just to see it sway with me, a feinting series of fluid dance steps, suspended in the water.

My child is smiling at me. He is a boy now, sturdy and strong. His bright smile lights up the dark places within me. But he is not looking at me. Instead, he looks past my shoulder into another world where he and I are strangers unrelated by blood or love.

He is a young man now, the light, fuzzy moustache on his upper lip contrasting with the tight control he keeps on his soft boyish mouth.

I see him as a man, a masculine, strong figure, with the soul of his father and the essence of my being shining through him.

But he and I are strangers forever and so shall we remain. I weep afresh at my loss and his.

How many useless dreams have I wasted away? How many times had I tried to tear through the curtain that had concealed this one secret from me? I had known my ultimate destiny but the loss of my child had been kept away from me, hidden, so I would do the bidding of my fate. Hidden so that I could not even hope to default on the debts of my past and the burden of my sins. And now he is gone… they are both gone from me… and I am trapped, swaying by my feet within the water hyacinth.

Chanda's laughter floats around and through me like a smooth current. She tells me, with glee, of the events still to come. I am not surprised and I give in to the soothing power of her mad voice. She tastes the salt of my tears and tells me she understands. I hear the muffled happy cries of her infant and for a moment I make believe he is mine. I know this is all an illusion. I had not helped her. I had let her die alone too. This has become the time of her retribution too. I am lost.

~

'You took my son,' I look straight into her eyes, my own blazing into hers with a terrible knowledge.

'You gave up your own son and now you have taken mine. You cannot have him.'

Gulbadan Begum looks at me like a bird caught by the mesmerizing gaze of a snake.

'I know. I know,' I tell her, my voice rising with each successive time I say those words, 'I know.' My mind is caught in an endless loop and cannot break away from the two words I keep repeating.

Her servants materialize out of nowhere and she shushes them away, as if afraid her secret will leak into the night and spread through the fort and the city like a malevolent spirit. She asks them to leave her rooms.

'What…' her voice is dry and she clears her throat. 'What are you talking about? My son… is dead. He was born dead like that poor woman's child who drowned in that lake. He is buried in Agra at the fort. I swear it. The pain… is so intense which is why I never talk of of him.'

'No, you are lying.' My shout reverberates inside the room. I continue.

'Her son died. Empress Hamida Banu's son died… he was born dead. You became pregnant at the same time as she did. She was too young. She was not used to that hard nomadic life and her child suffered from it. She never wanted to marry him… your beloved brother, Emperor Humayun. He was too old, too weak and set in his ways. The naked lust in his eyes repelled and terrified her. She loved another. But the emperor kept asking until her family could refuse him no longer. An emperor in exile is still an emperor and a beautiful daughter is a powerful bartering tool. So they accepted. But she did not want a child, her son born as a refugee, the poorest of the poor. She wanted her son to be born as the prince he was. She did not want to give birth on the run. So, she tried to get rid of her pregnancy but couldn't. Not until it was too late. The herbs she had taken had deformed her baby. He could not live outside her body. He took one breath in the open world, gasped and died.

'And then, as her dead son was laid in her arms, her unexpected, tortured grief came as a torrent. And she turned to you, her only friend and ally. She asked you for a favour. Together you made a deal as her son's body was enfolded into the ground. Your lifestyle… your life… would be guaranteed forever if you gave her your son. He would be the heir to the throne of Hindustan. He is your son, Emperor Akbar. That man who sits on the throne. I know this now. Give me back my son. Give him back and I will not tell anyone of this secret.'

Her crazed old-woman eyes are lucid and clear now. They stare at me intently through the veil of my flowing tears. 'You are insane. Your… your crazed mind tricked your body into believing… becoming pregnant. We have never seen anything like this. There was no child. You have no son. And now you are making up stories. Vicious, lying stories.' Her voice is strong and decisive and for a moment, just for a moment, I falter.

She is lying. Why are they all lying to me? Can they not see that I know the truth. I take a deep, shuddering breath and wipe away the streaming tears with the heels of my hands.

'Where have you hidden him? You give him back and I won't go to the emperor… to the people of the kingdom.' I have to use every weapon in my arsenal, everything I have. This is my only chance and I feel even it slipping away from me, like everything and everyone else in my life.

'You cannot go anywhere with these lies. No one will believe you. But I will give you what you want, whatever else you want.'

'I want my son.'

'There is no son.'

I know he is here, hidden somewhere, beautiful, perfect and mine. All I have left now that his father only visits me as mocking, harsh laughter in the dead of night. 'You killed me,' he tells me, refusing to believe my reasons, not listening to the story of his redemption. 'I tricked you like you betrayed me,' he laughs, 'revenge was long in coming. But you are finished now.'

'Finished,' I say aloud to myself. I know he speaks the truth.

'I want to stay here forever. I will wait for my son. He will find me here. And you,' I point to the old woman, 'you will stay here. They give you whatever you want. The empress promised you that. Tell them... him..., the emperor that you want to stay here with me. Tell them you need your solitude to write your history every day. And that means I will stay here too. I know now this is where I belong. This is where I was destined to live and to die.'

I do not wait for her answer. I do not need to.

I drink the salt of my tears as I make my way home and feel all the empty spaces in my life that my son and his father have violently torn open and left behind. The spaces that I fear will never be filled again.

My foreknowledge is a striking serpent, its cold tongue swirling inside my ear, telling me of things past and things to come. Its roughness slides up my body and dissolves into my skin, fading into the smooth vines of the water hyacinth that clambers up and holds me in its tight embrace. I give in.

Chanda laughs in the night, her voice like rippling water mingled with blood and tears.

19

City of Ghosts

Fatehpur Sikri, 1587

Each is a hidden treasure. Woody leather for skin, brown speckles on the red surface, hiding such tenderness, such sweetness, such juicy nectar within. I hold it in my hand, this fruit of secret beauty, the only symbol I have left of my love. I find my two loves within, for if I close my eyes as I bite into a single garnet seed of a ripe pomegranate I taste the keen longing for the Dom Raja and the intense love-pain I feel for my child. For that instant all three of us are connected, together. One.

My pomegranate tree has grown tall and when I stand under it, its leaves brush my face softly in a caress. Its blazingly red flowers scent the broken-down courtyard, wafting the perfume into my nose and making me remember those nights so long ago when the Dom Raja still visited me and made me feel whole, alive and not alone. Now the fruits are ripe, hanging tantalizingly low, ready to be plucked, living vehicles for my remembrance. When all others were lost to me I lavished my care on this tree, watering it, telling it tales of my life, letting the sharp need of my love seep into its roots.

I break a pomegranate open with my bare hands and watch as the thin, red juice spurts and runs down my hands and arms. Inside are nestled the tiny jewel-seeds, irresistable in their sweet crunchiness. I bring the broken half to my mouth and savagely tear into the fruit, not caring that the juices stain my clothes, smear my mouth and drip down my chin. I am starving for sweetness. When I bite into the fruit and feel keenly the presence of my love and my loss coexisting in the same space, for an instant the pain recedes. The pomegranate tree lives and it makes me feel alive, while the world around it dies painfully.

~

Fatehpur-Sikri is dying slowly, day by day, inch by inch. The stone-cutters of the original village of Sikri continue to thrive, travelling long distances to ply their trade wherever they can find work. They build mansions and houses, roads and inns, leaving their families behind as they seek their livelihood. Life has not changed much for them.

But the city of dreams, which once was the capital of the empire is wasting away before my eyes. The rough, dry dust mixed with sand from the terrain outside has begun to make inroads into the fort, eroding those fine palaces and deserted buildings that had once resonated with the power and majesty of governance.

The fountains are empty of water, and full instead of the earth that is reclaiming its lost territory. Tiny, hardy trees are growing from crevices, making them wider, the roots cracking through the stone, burrowing their way through the mortar, destroying the many years of labour, the vision of an emperor, his architects and artists. The walled city of Fatehpur-Sikri is peopled now only by the ghosts who still walk through its corridors and gardens and make their homes within these walls – them, and the many faithful who still visit the shrine of Sheikh Chishti. I, however, no longer visit his mausoleum or even his long-forgotten cave. I try to not even look in their direction. One night, a few years ago, I had crept inside his marble resting place to look upon the Sheikh's peaceful slumber. His tomb is shrouded under a rich, green velvet sheet embroidered in heavy gold. Over it is draped a webbed sheet of fragrant flowers, perfuming the night with a sweetness that mingles with the strong incense and makes me lightheaded.

I touch the marble-lace screen by which I had prayed so many nights, those years ago. Such futility. The swinging shadows from the hanging lamp cast dark, mobile shapes on my skin. My fingers feel their way through the many pieces of thread until I find my lock of hair. I untie the strong knot that I had tied with so much fervour and hope. I feel the once-living fibres tear and disintegrate within my strong grasp. I hold it for a moment, dry and brittle, on one palm, and then crumble it into black dust. Once I am outside I open my hand again and blow these pieces of myself into the inky night. The particles mingle with the sand, the darkness and the emptiness.

The ghost of an emperor's capricious vision too haunts the majestic buildings. Some nights as I wander through the darkened rooms I can still hear his applause and words of praise as he enjoyed the sound of Andaliib's peerless, throaty voice. From the periphery of my vision I can see her scars, some silver like tiny fish, others dark like knotted ropes.

The thunder of his voice as he delivered verdicts or addressed his courtiers still echoes in the confines of red sandstone and marble. I can hear the battle of wits that had raged in the Ibadatkhana, the pleas brought to the halls of public audience, the shouted orders and commands that had made this whole place operate. In the once-abundant gardens, the trees are gnarled, thirsty or dead, the flowers decimated, the channels that had once gurgled with water are now choked with dust. The rivers of life are clogged with soil and weeds.

My son lives here, in me, but he is no ghost. He is a live, vital presence and I mark the passage of his years in my heart and on my body. Each year that we have been apart is one stroke of my knife upon my skin. I am sure he will find me here some day. So I talk to him still, repeating to him my stories so that he will recognize my voice. I close my eyes and bring him to my presence so that he will know my smell. My heart is timed to his. We beat together in rhythm. My heart will know him and the hunger of my soul shall be sated when I see him stand before me.

His father haunts me now only in my dreams. His voice beckons me from among the flowers of the water hyacinth, so loud and insistent that it drowns out the sounds of my childhood. I realize now that he loves me still for if he did not he would have long ago left my presence. No, despite, his anger and betrayal he loves me. . I am his addiction, his black desire, the twisted object of his fascination. He is drawn to me even though he hates me. What can that be but love? I am glad; I thrill to the brunt of his dark emotions and hear his mocking, hurtful laughter when he talks to me. As long as he is around me I know I am not alone.

~

It has been years since the emperor left for Punjab, so many years that I have lost count. Time means nothing any more at Fatehpur-Sikri. . I wait for snippets of news from the world outside Fatehpur-Sikri to filter back to me, from travellers passing through, stone-cutters returning from faraway places. The last I had heard, many years ago, the emperor had crossed the river Sutlej and set up camp in Lahore, directing his campaign of expansion and consolidation. During his absence the empress had kept the royal messengers busy delivering her long letters to him. He had written back often, telling her of the many sights he saw, of the battles he won, of his wounds and victories. His words would reach us months later, filtered through the many layers of people between her and us.

Then one day, five years after his departure, a letter had arrived, the one she had been waiting for, the fruition of all her gentle written manipulations. In letter after letter to him she had hinted in roundabout ways that perhaps they should be reunited. That perhaps Fatehpur-Sikri was not the best place for their capital. That it did not make strategic sense in light of his growing conquests and the expansion of the empire.

And now here it was, finally, a summons for her to leave Fatehpur-Sikri and to join the emperor at his fort in Lahore. Prince Salim had already been sent to lead an army of expansion. They would all be reunited and Chanda's curse would remain directed towards the fort and the dying city as her human prey crept quietly away. The empress called me to her presence.

'Soothsayer, I want to thank you for warning me. Because of you my family shall live, the kingdom shall survive. What can I do for you?' the empress asked, looking at my face for the first time.

'Give me back my son.'

'There was no son,' she replied, looking away, but the kindness in her voice seeped through her words like a cooling balm that soothed and annoyed me. Her revulsion for me had been swept away in a flood of relief and perhaps even pity. I could sense that.

'Then, let me remain here… forever… for as long as I live. Provide for me until the end of my days. That is all I ask.'

'Ask for more, something better, soothsayer. We… I owe you more. Riches, jewels, a grander house. Ask.'

'You cannot give me what I truly want. And I want nothing else.' By giving me things she sought to right the balance that had been shifted in my favour. She wanted to buy my services as befitted an empress, rather than getting the benefit of my foreknowledge for no price. Royalty cannot be indebted to anyone.

'Perhaps, once everyone has left the city I… I can move into the fort.' My little home had of late been too full of the lost possibilities of my life. It was the home I had built for my son, the place I had envisioned I would grow old in. But my recreation of Zameerpur was after all just a mirage, an empty shell save for the pomegranate tree.

She had no choice but to grant me my wish. It was the last time I would see her.

She departed a few days later and I moved into one of the empty palaces within the fort. Except for the servants, only Gulbadan Begum and I remain in the fort. I keep her secret safe, hidden away like a powerful weapon. She never tells me about my son or what happened to him. Each night she dreams. Each day I write. I, Nadee, have been ordained the keeper of the secrets of this fort and city; the writer of its chronicles.

The tome is thick now and grows every day. I write, as she tells me, of the intrigues within the zenana, the infidelities, the indelicate liaisons, the lies. I listen as she details the fears and torments of the newly arrived members of the harem, after being torn away from their families, pawns in the game of building an empire and making friends of enemies and rivals. These fragile links, tools of nascent political alliances come alive under Gulbadan Begum's telling, filling our empty days. The jealousies and bickerings of the emperor's wives and concubines as they fought for his limited time, come through to me in waves of sound, through pictures drawn with words, through the silences and what was left unsaid. The news of various victories that she had heard about, the onward march of the Mughal Empire, and the history of valiant, hardy, warrior-emperors were all told from a distance, from behind the seclusion of her veil.

Outside, between the village of Sikri and the fort-city, lies Fatehpur Lake and Chanda. Chanda senses the emptiness of the fort and is ecstatic with victory. She thinks she has won. She, Chanda, has destroyed a city, a capital and an emperor. In a way, perhaps she has. The hollowness of her incomplete victory eludes her, however. She is so blind with the knowledge of her power that she does not see that she herself is being destroyed. She is weak, spent of the power she had gained when she had first died.

The seed that she dropped into the lake has grown into a mighty plant that is choking the surface of the water. And it is destroying her with it. Fatehpur Lake is half of what it used to be. The banks are now just a wreath of leaves, vines and flowers. The centre is a stubborn island of water that stands steadfast against the onslaught of its own inevitable defeat. Our servants have had to dig deep wells to get enough water for our needs from this hard-baked land. The lake is unusable, its water stale, brown and undrinkable.

Chanda's voice is growing weaker, fainter, as if she talks and laughs and plots from a great distance, weakening with each instant that passes. She does not recognize her loosening grip, so ferocious is her hatred. She is blind and deaf to all else.

The roads between Agra and Fatehpur-Sikri are overgrown with vegetation since they fell into disuse years ago. The howling wind echoes a plaintive, wailing song through the rooms of the empty garrisons and stables.

Sometimes, when I climb to the top storey of the paanch mahal I look into the inn. Where once it used to be filled to capacity it is now almost empty. There is little need for most traders and merchants to come to Fatehpur-Sikri. I cast my eyes into the interior of the fort and see the onslaught of slow decay setting in. The halls and corridors that had once been full of people, ringing with important pronouncements and great decisions are now echoingly empty. In the distance I glimpse the tiny, silver platter which is all that is left of the lake glimmering, struggling to shine in the weak light.

~

Chanda's laughter is weak. She sounds exhausted and her triumph has begun to sour. Now that Fatehpur-Sikri is empty and the emperor has departed, she no longer has a purpose. I am afraid that all her hatred and bile is coalescing into a torrent and pointing towards me. To her, I am the last one. The last symbol, a link to the once prosperous and alive capital city of Fatehpur-Sikri. And I, the only one with the ability to hear her, had not tried to help her when she had stumbled past me in the dark to her lonely, watery death. She and her infant son had drowned; she is now convinced, because of me. I am the only one left here and so I must be made accountable. I sense her turn her gaze on me and feel her hatred like a vicious slap, her vengeance like a scorpion's sting.

I plead out my explanations for her, telling her about that night, about my life. But she mocks me, laughing at my pain, relishing the torment I relive every day through the retribution of the Dom Raja and the loss of my precious son. My pain is her only comfort. She is happy that I suffer.

I am tired of her constant presence, her selective hearing and understanding, her myopic awareness of my life. Tired of her laughter that makes fun of my tears and of the futile grasping of my dreams. Tired. Each day I walk to the lake to see how much water remains, as the water hyacinth marches on in triumph, weaving a living carpet. And when the lake is finally gone, so will she be. The knowledge of that gives me some comfort.

~

I lie on the hard ground, feeling the flat, smooth, cool stones of the empty courtyard on my back. If I turn my head I can see the mausoleum of the Sheikh, its lights casting dancing shadows in the night.

It is at night that the ghosts of the city walk freely through it. And I watch them hurry by, unmindful of my presence, just as they had been in life and in reality. I hear their conversations, eavesdrop on their intrigues as I think of the history I am writing.

'I have more power than you know.' I whisper the words into the night and not one of the ghosts hears me. They exist in a place away from me.

I laugh then, aloud. The sound echoes through the empty courtyard, where the mosque stands majestic and darkened and the marble mausoleum glows in the moonlight. My echoes return to me, piercing my ears, unstopping until I cannot bear the sound any more. Gradually, they fade away, melting into the distant dark.

Soon it will be time. I wait.

20

Nadee: River of Life

Fatehpur Lake, 1599

I am Nadee, the river of life. I was known once by another name but like many others have in my life, that memory too has receded into the deep, treacherously swirling currents of my past. This past still haunts me like a shiver caused by a sudden cold wind, coming upon me at unexpected times and always without warning. My life has meandered through the passages of history, carrying me along, powerless and frightened, trying to maintain some control, gain some mastery over it. No longer; no longer am I a mute witness, a mad woman, a soothsayer in the service of an emperor, a killer, a childless mother, a loverless woman.

I am a river, of mystery and sorrow, powerful and yielding, life-giving and life-taking. I see myself now, separate from what is said about me, away from the whispers, away from the guiles and dangerous suggestions of Ganga, away from the tepid friendship of Yamuna, away from the city in which I live now. I see who I am. I have killed and I have given life. I have told truths and many lies. I have railed against my fate and been trapped by it, its tentacles digging so deep into me that they merge into the very veins that run through my body. I have survived. Above all else, I have survived. I am here.

Weavers have incorporated my likeness into carpets and emperors have tried to recreate my disordered chaos into contained channels of stone to water their gardens of paradise. Artists have tried to paint my essence on to paper, with colour and imagination. The river of life to them is sparkling, a blue ribbon of water, pure and fresh. It is all illusion. They are fools, all of them.

'You cannot grasp me. You cannot catch me. You cannot predict the directions in which I flow. You cannot count the colours of the rainbows that burst out of my surface when the sun hits my waters just right. You cannot plumb my depths. You cannot meet me and emerge unscathed.' This I shout into the barren wilderness at night and feel my words, like drops of water, fly back in the wind and splash against my face. I taste salt on my lips.

I had a task. A task I had asked for and taken on of my own will. It was my destiny, whispered to me by my foreknowledge. I was to be the pen through which the history of Gulbadan Begum's ancestors was to be written. She had written down the dreams of her past, tracing her path as a young wife and mother. I was to write the rest. I was to write of the glorious triumphs of the Great Mughals, the campaigns of her brother and nephew – her son – of life behind the guarded walls of the only world she had ever known.

I have betrayed that task. I floundered for a while, writing down Gulbadan Begum's words, and then gave in to something else, calling to me from within myself. Myself. For some time now as she had talked to me in her shaded and delicate Persian, and the ink from my quill had flowed in black rivulets across the paper, I had tricked her. She was old and almost blind now. She could barely make out the black letters that danced on the page. If she could have read them she would have been enraged. For I was no longer writing the history of the great Mughals. I had waylaid the history of another and infused it with my own story.

I am writing my history. I could not help myself. I tried to keep true to my task, to adhere to the burden and the demands of history. But they all paled in comparison to the story of my own life. My story drowns out the sound of my own voice that echoes in my ears and forces me to write what I must. History seems a cold, bloodless dead thing in contrast. There are many who are writing about the emperor and his reign. Generations to follow shall know him and his ancestors. But I am nameless. Unknown and alone. Who would write about me, if not I?

So, even as Gulbadan Begum's shaky, aging voice painted landscapes of events and portraits of greatness, the words that emerged from my soul and gained form on paper were mine, mine alone. Each letter that crawled like a fast-moving, black insect onto the parchment was torn from the depths of my self.

I was a child when my journey began, petulant, impetuous and bursting with unharnessed energy. I was the daughter of farmers from the village of Zameerpur before I became the river of life. Not a life-giving river, but one in which many lives were, are and will be lived.

Over the years, I have carved my story into my skin but now I realize that it is an impermanent canvas. It will perish with me. Who will know me then? I know that stories that are written on paper survive and so shall mine. I am compelled to leave a trace, to not be forgotten, to live on somehow. I am obsessed with this work I must do.

Once I saw the phases of my life in weak flickers of interrupted light. I knew the beginning and I could clearly see the end of my path. But what lay in between? Each tiny, sporadic burst of illumination showed me just my next step, foretold what was just about to happen, leaving large parts in darkened shadows. I move, unsurprised, from event to event, yet always shaken, never not on-edge. Not quite knowing all.

I spoke truths that foreshadowed destinies. I have lived many lifetimes since Ganga swept me away from my birth-home. Like all rivers, I am a vagabond, never living in one place for too long. I have flowed through the passages of history and have left faint marks of my existence that time shall undoubtedly erase. Unless I do something about it. It is my responsibility.

~

Other rivers are goddesses, divine daughters, all-powerful deities. I am mortal and flawed, the offspring of anonymous mediocrity. In a parallel destiny I would have been a farmer's wife, like Chanda. Unlike her, I would have had many children. Strong sons who would have imbued me with their power and the strength of their devotion, giving me status in society. Daughters in whose girlish ways I would have forgotten my own advancing years.

These are the children whose faces I had drawn madly every day until the reality of my true son invaded every part of my being. Upon my death, my eldest son would have lit my funeral pyre and many would have cried. Perhaps my ashes would have been taken to Kashi and merged with the waters of Ganga. Death flowing into life; life flowing through death. All becoming one. That was not to be, however.

Instead, I went to Kashi as a frightened, wandering refugee, saved by the vagaries of the very river who had destroyed my past. Kashi, the city of the dead was where I had found a love that had overcome all boundaries and gone beyond all limits. The city, wreathed in smoke and the smell of burning humanity had invaded every sense, blotted my reason and helped make me who I am today.

Killer whirlpools and powerfully playful eddies swirl within me, making my pasts collide with my present and mesh seamlessly into the future that looms towards me, ominous and inescapable. The future is a giant fall that will suck my waters down with great force and spit them out with devastating power, shattering them on to the rocks of life. I know. I know. It is time and yet I am afraid. I can see the end this day, as clear as dawn, but still something buried deep within me stirs my cowardice.

I am powerless despite the buried strength that makes me go on. I write my history, every day, on paper and on skin, using ink and blood. I draw and re-draw the face of my son. Shadowed within his features is the face of his father. Two into one. One into two. Where does one end and the other begin? Where do I end and they begin?

I have traversed tributaries of blood, bound by duty and destiny to the greatest courtesan of her age. I have used my burden – which many consider a gift – in the service of the greatest emperor that history has known. I have experienced the agony of a woman who has lost her child and her life. All this was not for nothing. For brief moments, short bursts, I gained the seduction of being needed, and of status and reprieve, and a home. A home, a house I could call my own, perfumed with the winsome, young blossoms of the pomegranate tree. Pomegranates that tasted of love. A fort and palaces that were meant to house only royalty.

~

Gulbadan Begum is dead. Gradually, so silently that her passing might not have registered at all. Nothing remarkable about her death except that her nephew has returned to personally carry her bier on his shoulder. The King of the World wept openly as he helped her make her last journey. He has come back to Fatehpur-Sikri after many years. He has come as a stranger, as an observer. He feels an un-nameable loss that he cannot comprehend, a jumble of emotions that go far beyond the bonds that tie an aunt and a nephew, a monarch and his doomed vision. As the years pass he may ponder this but the need to examine these feelings will pass with time and fade into his past.

He does not come alone. He has brought with him a small entourage to help make his stay comfortable. I come into his presence and it takes him a moment to remember me. Time has erased the immediacy of his memories, dulled the emotions that had brought me to his attention so long ago. Time has sprinkled my hair with white and etched creases into my skin. He is kind and polite. He assures me that I can stay on in Fatehpur-Sikri for as long as I want, while also letting me know that there will always be a place for me in his court should I desire to rejoin it some day. I thank him and depart from this presence. I know that I am seeing him for the last time. I know that he will die this day, five years from now. I do not tell him this, for he has to meet his final destiny by himself, on his own terms and in his own time.

~

For long moments sometimes, if I close my eyes, I can drift away into the past of the city, when it was still vibrant, youthful and important. I hear the voices of his serving men and women as I slip comfortably unnoticed through their ranks. The emperor's arrival, temporary though it is, has reanimated this dying place.

The fort is alive again with the sights, the sounds and the smells of royalty. I pretend this will last forever. Not many people of his entourage notice a prematurely greying woman, growing older than her years. I am seeking news, some information. I sift through their words and uncover the nugget of treasure for which I have been looking.

~

I try to listen for news of my son. He is fully grown, almost. If I said aloud the words that are burning with impatience on my tongue everyone would laugh at me: Khusro is the name of my son. Gulbadan Begum would have told me I was mad, deranged. How could my son be a prince? Prince Khusro? His name tastes sweet in my mouth when I roll it on my tongue and whisper it out aloud to myself. Khusro! A beautiful name, one I might have chosen for him myself. I repeat it often, like a delightful secret. Gulbadan Begum would have told me that the timing is wrong, the calculations impossible, the very thought preposterous. But a mother is not wrong. She knows. I know.

The world knows young Prince Khusro as the son of Prince Salim. I hear of his exploits, his kindness and his gentleness and the greatness that blazes like the sun from his countenance. I know he is mine. I know, too, his destiny.

I know his father's love for me is displayed in flashes that often feel like hatred. Yet his dark emotions pulse and throb around me with an intensity that can only be love. He is proud of his son. I know it. He – the Dom Raja, King of the Dead – is father to a Mughal prince. And not just any prince, but Khusro, whom people in the streets already compare to his iconic grandfather, Akbar. He is also the Khusro, whom history will remember with remote kindness, as an afterthought, as one who could have been great. The knowledge of his fate gushes into me on a wave of sadness. I feel my heart begin to cave in on itself and my protective instincts rise up within me like a rushing waterfall.

He has all the marks of greatness, I hear. He is popular, more loved than his father by the people, and the favourite of his aging grandfather. There are rumours that Emperor Akbar may bypass his mercurial, rebellious son and leave the throne to the young prince Khusro instead.

Khusro, my son, you were meant to be an emperor. Yes, I can see that in you. That is your destiny... is one of your possible destinies. Destiny is an errant river at the mercy of circumstance, luck and decisions that cannot be unmade. Its currents run deep and strong, trapping the unwitting, the naïve and the unaware. They coalesce into whirling waters of other times and through the actions of other people. My son, you were born to a murderer, a mad woman, and you carry her sins upon your unblemished soul. My sins and the sins carried through generations on your father's side... your true father.

'Khusro...' my heart screams out aloud across the miles, '...listen. Your destiny is what you make of it. Be patient. Do not give in to those thoughts of rebellion that shadow your mind. Do not believe you are invincible. You are still a prince, not yet an emperor. Do not over-step your bounds. The paths which you are traversing are meandering and treacherous. Be careful. Stop!' I see into his future for one long frightening moment, his life laid bare in front of me, and I feel the blood congeal in my veins.

'But you cannot hear me. You are too far away and your mother's words slide away from you like drops of water in a strong wind. Drops that evaporate into nothingness, burned away in the heat of the sun of ambition and power and your pre-written destiny. I do not know how to reach you, how to make you listen.

'I shall be your witness too, Khusro. This history I write is yours, as well. I write it with hope. Hope that what I sense about your eventual fate is false. Hope that everything I see about the man you will be, is true. Hope that you will twist apart the intertwined destinies of your parents and tear them asunder, freeing yourself in the process. Hope that you will become someone the world has never seen. Hope that you will surpass greatness. Hope that you will carve out your own destiny and not fall prey to the sadistic vagaries of fate.

'Learn from my life, Khusro and be made wise. Look upon the meandering, lost path of my life and understand the realities that I could neither fully see nor grasp. I was caught, trapped in a maelstrom of my own making and of my burden. I could not see. But you can. You can see the whole of me, from source to end, as I could not at the beginning of my journey. You can see every decision, every bend, every rapid, every action, every thought, every feeling. You have the perspective of distance and remoteness. Learn your lessons well, Khusro.'

I am nearing the end of my own journey. I hear the roar of the falling water as I rush towards it. I have no will left, no choice. A part of me is still not ready. It refuses to accept, refuses to give in. 'That part is you Khusro. The mother-part that cannot fully leave until she sees you and holds you once in her arms, feels the warmth of your skin, the silk of your hair, feels our beating hearts together at last.' In the midst of all, I have comforting knowledge.

'Comfort that I will not be alone. Your father will always be with me. Lover or fiend, vengeance seeker or friend, perpetrator or victim, refuge or betrayer; we are all these and more to each other. Every emotion, every half-shaded, indistinct feeling pulsates within and between us.'

~

Gushing water; a boiling, mad beast. It raises its voice higher every second until the sound fills my ears and forces everything else out of the way. I am pushed closer. Fatehpur Lake's destiny it is to be an eternal, mystical sea that lies outside the realm of what man can see. I carry my history with me. It is my anchor, my connection to my journey thus far and beyond.

The shore is crumbling. Hard rocks, crusty brown earth. My foot slips. A rock scrapes it. I bleed. I smile. Blood trails like fragile, red lace. Outlines of my foot on the hard earth in red. Dark, lighter, lightest, faint… gone.

I am here.

Young vines are pliant. I push them out of the way with my one free hand. The other clutches my book. I walk deeper. My clothes fill with stinking, rancid water and float up around my waist. The vines are tougher now, smooth and woody, inflexible. Strong. Determined.

Chanda whispers, 'You are here at last. I was waiting. I am lonely... all alone. You are my friend.' She sounds like a frightened child who cannot breathe, whose voice is being choked, the life draining out of her. She has become one with her son.

'Yes,' I whisper back. I swallow my tears. Briny. Wet. They taste of my past. I drink them down, slaking my thirst.

The ground plunges into nothingness beneath my feet. I am close to the centre. In the one place where all lives intersect, all people, all loves. Everything. My fingers slip, relaxing their grip, and meet water.

The pages float away. One by one. Waterlogged. Ink bleeds into the water, sodden paper disintegrates, dissipates into the surrounding water, becoming part of the landscape. Becoming one with it. Immutable and unerasable.

I trace the name my parents had given me, the name I had not heard for so many years. It connects me, for an instant, to the time before my journey had begun. I warm my hand on the healed gash on my left side that I had made for the Dom Raja. My past, my present and my future mesh together and I feel a peace creep over me.

My lover's strong arms hold me tight. My son caresses my cheek with velvet palms, and I feel his warm breath wash over me like a balm. He is here. I had known he would find me. His heart is pressed against mine. We beat in the same rhythm, the same timing. I close my eyes and savour this moment of oneness with my son. My parents' voices sound relieved and joyful. They have been waiting the longest for me. They have been calling me for years, since we parted, and now I am here, finally here.

The voices from my past mesh with those from my present. A fast-whirling, deep pool lies still, in the centre. In the centre there is calm. I am past the waterfall now. To the confluence that is my destiny. The one place where all meets nothing and transforms both. Changes all.

'Yes, I am here. At last I am here.' I speak my response to those voices aloud and in a firm voice. I laugh and my laughter ripples with a deep cadence.

The flower petals stroke my skin like satin fingers. The vines wind their way around my body gently. I do not sense their tightening as pain. I feel comforted and secure, held in a tight, loving embrace. Peace. I see the grey-brown earth and the azure-flecked-with-white skies as my eyes slip slowly under the surface. They… we are all here. The two rivers flow towards me, their conflicting waters meeting in a sigh of silence, as I swim into them.

~

A large purple flower blooms in the exact centre of the dry-caked muck in the middle of the arid depression in the ground that was once Fatehpur Lake.